The Mystery of the Ark
Allen Schery

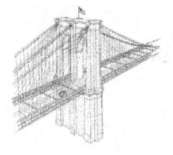

Brooklyn Bridge Books

Copyright © 2025 by Allen Schery

Registration number TXu 2-502-601

All rights reserved.

ISBN 978-1-968950-00-2

No portion of this book may be reproduced in any form without written permission from the publisher or author, except as permitted by U.S. copyright law.

DEDICATION

John Stephen Kopper 1923-1984

I dedicate this book to true Archeologists, not movie varieties like Indiana Jones who romantically portrays an image that does not exist. From personal experience I can attest that excess heat, poor water and food along with difficult places to sleep while scorpions dance by one's head. On most mornings a tarp has to be removed from the dig while having to eliminate spiders and snakes that found warmth overnight. Many of these were poisonous. I lost one third of my weight while pursuing that goal in the Yucatan in the early 1970's. I created this fertile novel from my archeological and historical interests. It is a mystery fortified with knowledge gleaned from those experiences laced with Hitchcockian McGuffins to purposely mislead. Our hero archeologist Steve Kopper was a real-life archeologist who majored in megalithic Balearic Islands Archeology, He introduced me to Archeology in 1968 at Post College. He died at age 61 in 1984 caused by pipe smoking and is buried at Calverton National Cemetery on Long Island 3000 miles from where I now sit. This is my small way of remembering and thanking him.

Contents

1. On Patmos — 1
2. On to Rhodes — 10
3. On to Qumran — 20
4. The Meeting — 30
5. The Chamber of Whispers — 41
6. Dawn of Reckoning — 51
7. From Ponza to Rome — 61
8. The Light of Judgment — 72
9. The Last Bell — 81
10. The Red Mustang — 86
11. Dawn on the Shasta Trails — 92
12. The Dry River of Gold — 99
13. On the Gold Road — 105
14. Purposeful Evil — 110
15. Whispers from Rosslyn Chapel — 116

16.	Two Close for Comfort	121
17.	The Shaking Earth	128
18.	The Choking Whisper	134
19.	The Levis's Golden Seraphim Wings	140
20.	The Electric Wings Spark	146
About the Author		155
Index		157

Chapter One
On Patmos

Patmos, the smallest and northernmost of the original twelve Dodecanese islands, lay adrift in the Aegean Sea—a solitary sentinel caught between the winds of history and the whispers of myth. Its jagged, arc-shaped silhouette, hewn by the fury of a prehistoric volcano, rose defiantly against a roiling twilight sky. The island's contours were raw and uncompromising, shaped by nature's capricious hand into three deeply indented headlands bound together by two slender isthmuses, fragile threads tethering an ageless relic to the pulse of the present.

The terrain was at once barren and magnetic—a harsh canvas on which time had painted both desolation and allure. Rugged hills, smoothed only by the relentless caress of winds and salt, bore the scars of millennia. Against a backdrop of endless blue, ancient ruins clung to these hillsides like stubborn memories. To the north, the remains of an acropolis stood—a weathered monument to Artemis Patmia, once revered as the island's fierce protector. Now, with the passage of time and the arrival of darker deities, her name had dwindled to a barely audible murmur—a lament carried on the salt-laden breezes that swept the land.

Amid this wilderness of stone and memory, a solitary cave beckoned—a natural vault deep in the earth that seemed to hoard both the weight of the past and the fragile hopes of the present. Exiled here by the unyielding decree of the Roman emperor Nero, John had made the cave his reluctant sanctuary. The cavern's walls, rough and timeworn, bore silent testimony to the relentless drip of water over centuries, crafting delicate streaks through the darkness. Here, in the chill of abandonment, every echo resonated with both sorrow and defiance.

That late afternoon, as the failing light surrendered to encroaching gloom, the storm began its subtle arrival. A faint breeze—playful at first—skipped over the narrow isthmuses, stirring the dry, briny air and hinting at the tempest to come. Slowly, the gentle whisper spiraled into a wild, cacophonous roar—as if the ancient gods themselves had taken to the skies. The wind, once a delicate murmur, now howled like a spectral beast, tearfully lashing at the jagged cliffs and clawing at the entrance of John's cave with spectral, icy fingers.

Rain erupted in torrents, each drop a shard of biting ice striking the barren terrain. The air filled with the rhythmic drum of raindrops meeting stone and sand, creating a tumultuous symphony that resonated with primal urgency. Beyond the rocky shoreline, the darkened sea churned violently. Immense, frothing waves crashed against the cliffs with a deafening might, echoing like ancient drums in a forgotten battle. Lightning fractured the sky into fleeting moments of blinding brilliance—each flash briefly revealing the wild, sculpted drama of the island—before the thunder rolled in deep, resonant growls that shook the very foundations of the earth.

Inside his cave, John awoke with a sudden, jarring start. His heart pounded in his ears as if it were trying to drown out the tumult outside. Clutching the coarse, damp fabric of his worn tunic, he sought anchorage in this familiar tactile comfort. In a moment when the boundary between sleep and waking blurred, harrowing visions returned—spectral apparitions that invaded his mind with the ferocity of the storm outside. In his dreams, a furious conflagration rained from the heavens, devouring mountains and seas in an unstoppable inferno. Angels clad in radiant armor clashed with swirling, demonic silhouettes as celestial blades of light cut through layers of shadow. The very earth ruptured, and streams of molten fire snaked like living serpents between crumbling ravines. Over it all, an unearthly chorus of voices cried out in despairing cacophony that vibrated through his bones.

John pressed his back against the cold, uneven wall of the cave, his wide, unseeing eyes reflecting the horrors that had invaded his soul. The storm's ferocity seemed to have seeped into every fiber of his being, mingling with the spectral whispers that threaded through his mind in a language older than time. Their message—inevitable and profound—spoke of an impending end. "The end... it is near," he uttered, his voice a trembling whisper barely audibles above the tempest. "The world will burn, and all shall be unmade." In that charged moment, tears—cold, unyielding, born of despair—traced silent paths down his weathered face, each drop an echo of a sorrow too deep for mortal measure.

He had borne exile and solitude for so long that physical isolation had become almost bearable. Yet these visions were of a different order—a despair so overwhelming it felt as if his very soul were being fractured, split open and exposed to the relentless bite of fate. Outside, the storm raged as if it were less a collision of natural elements and more an incarnation of divine wrath. The air around the cave grew even colder, and the dancing shadows on the walls deepened, as though the darkness itself were swallowing the fragile remnants of light.

Time became an abstract notion in the chaos of that tormented night. Whether hours or mere moments elapsed, the relentless fury of the storm gradually ebbed into a somber refrain. The torrential downpour diminished to a mournful patter, as if the heavens themselves were weeping softly over lost dreams. The wind, once a terrified howl, subsided to a whisper—a final, reluctant sigh of resignation—and the sea, though still restless, receded to a distant murmur that belied the lingering threat.

Exhaustion overtook John. He slumped onto the rough cave floor, his limbs heavy as if weighed down by fate itself. His breathing, though eventually steadying, could not dispel the ghostly whispers that wove through his mind, persistent and insistent, carrying fragments of an unfathomable truth as crushing as the hand of destiny. Sleep reclaimed him—not with the gentle embrace of respite, but as a restless sojourn into a dreamscape both bleak and beckoning.

In that troubled sleep, John journeyed through barren, twilight landscapes where shadows whispered secrets and ancient ruins loomed like specters. He meandered along paths illuminated by an unearthly light—a light that revealed mysterious symbols etched into weathered stone and hidden alcoves holding crumpled scrolls, their faded ink hinting at prophecies lost to time. Amid twisted groves of gnarled olive trees, a pale beacon beckoned him forward, a silent promise of st amid the ruin.

When at last he awoke, the first delicate fingers of dawn crept into the cave like tender brushstrokes upon cold stone. Hues of lavender and pink blush softened the jagged walls, gradually banishing the brutal scars left by the raging night. The air, infused with the fresh tang of dewy earth and a subtle perfume of sea spray, promised renewal in stark contrast to the tempest's earlier venom.

John rose with deliberate care, each movement a silent protest against the lingering chill embedded in his bones. As he emerged from the dark sanctuary, his senses were bathed anew in the island's vivid morning splendor. The rugged rocks, damp with the residue of night's fury, shimmered in the gentle light. Every crevice held rivulets of water that sparkled with a purity born of renewal, while the soft, bracing aroma of wild herbs and salt mingled with the faint floral notes drifting from unseen blossoms.

Stepping away from the cave, John found himself in a transformed world. The once hellish chaos of the storm gave way to a landscape of raw, unfiltered beauty. In the distance, the ruins of the ancient acropolis of Artemis Patmia loomed—a skeletal reminder of glory and loss. Its crumbling columns and shattered altars, bathed in the early warmth of the sun, exuded an ineffable melancholy. The place was steeped in an aroma of aged stone mingled with the lingering trace of incense—a spectral reminder of rituals long abandoned.

With measured steps, John traversed a narrow, weathered path that wound its way toward the ruins. Every footfall produced a soft, gravelly crunch over worn stones, each sound resonating as though marking the footnotes of a bygone era. As he neared the acropolis, the tactile sensation of rough-hewn stone beneath his fingertips rekindled memories of ancient prayers and sacred chants. The soft rustling of the wind amid the remnants of moss and lichen on the crumbling edifice felt like a celestial hymn—a delicate chorus of nature in quiet mourning.

There, in the silence of that sacred space, memories flooded back with an intensity that blurred the boundaries of time. Reminders of a life once brimming with purpose intertwined with the bitter solitude of exile. In that moment, John questioned the price of destiny and the inscrutable design that had led him to this forlorn isle. Was his isolation a cruel punishment, or rather a divinely orchestrated trial designed to unlock hidden truths and awaken a long-dormant spirit?

The sound of the wind—soft, sibilant whispers that seemed to echo ancient incantations—mingled with the rhythmic pulse of the earth beneath his feet. Each gust carried with it the elemental perfume of myrrh and the salt of distant seas, evoking images of long-forgotten ceremonies and fervent devotion. In that hallowed silence, every natural voice, the gentle lapping of the calm sea, the distant cry of a lone seabird, even the whisper of his own heartbeat coalesced into a singular, resonant message: the present was but a prelude to an unfolding prophecy.

Resolved to embrace the path forged in dreams and heralded by storm, John retrieved a small, timeworn journal from the depths of his satchel. Its leather cover was softened by years of handling, its brittle pages inscribed with cryptic musings and half-forgotten prophecies. With quiet determination, he set off once more into the rugged embrace of Patmos, each step imprinted with the memory of past anguish and the flicker of nascent hope.

Climbing a gentle rise that offered a commanding view over the island, he beheld the full, wild tapestry of Patmos. Jagged cliffs plunged dramatically into the ever-restless Aegean, while scattered clusters of hardy shrubs and wind-whipped pines clung to life amid the stone. The low murmur of the receding storm mingled with the subtle susurrations of awakening nature, crafting a melody of both lament and promise.

In that contemplative moment, John's inner voice, tempered by both despair and defiant hope, spoke of renewal. The visions of fiery cataclysms and celestial battles, though harrowing, had unveiled an undeniable truth: every end bore the seed of its own beginning. The very elements—earth, wind, water, and fire—seemed to conspire in this crucible of fate, intertwining his destiny with the ancient rhythms of the land.

Thus, beneath an expansive sky gradually reclaiming its cobalt depth, John resolved to journey deeper into the heart of the island—and into the mysteries that wove together myth, memory, and destiny. With each deliberate step along the narrow, winding paths and through the hallowed ruins of a once-sacred civilization, he embraced the fragrance of dew-soaked earth, the caress of a cooling breeze, and the timeless whispers of stones that had witnessed the rise and fall of empires.

In the quiet majesty of that transformative dawn, Patmos revealed itself not merely as a place of exile, but as a living testament to the enduring interplay of destruction and rebirth. And as the muted light of morning bathed the island in hopeful gold, John's heart, scarred yet resolute, beat in rhythm with the ancient pulse of the earth—a steady cadence that affirmed his place in the eternal, unfolding saga of time.

So began his pilgrimage—not just across a wild, untamed island, but into the very heart of a destiny foretold. For in every shattered ruin and every gust of wind murmuring forgotten secrets, he sensed the promise of an awakening, a renewal that would ripple through the ages, forever altering the tapestry of both his soul and the world around him.

Chapter Two
On to Rhodes

Under a gentle blush of dawn on Patmos, Pliny's weathered vessel, its hull salt-crusted and time-honored, glided steadily toward the weathered quay. Unlike any boat John had ever flown his own colors on, this craft bore the unmistakable mark of its master—a testament to countless journeys and storied harbors. John, driven by a desire not merely to travel but to be part of something greater, had come to seek his passage: to secure a position on Pliny's crew and join him on the fabled voyage toward Rhodes.

Stepping off the gangway, John's keen eyes met those of the man whose life had been woven with the threads of adventure. Pliny stood near the vessel, his stance both commanding and weathered, as if the sea itself had sculpted his every line. In the soft morning air—tangled with the scent of brine, wild thyme, and the promise of discovery—John dared to introduce himself. "I have come seeking a chance to join a journey worth remembering," he said quietly, his tone imbued with both hope and humble determination.

Pliny's gaze, deep and searching as the ocean, flickered with a quiet acknowledgment. "Many have sought passage on this ship," he began, his voice low and measured, "but few possess both the spirit and resolve to bear witness to the mysteries that await beyond these familiar shores. Rhodes is no mere destination—it is a realm where the echoes of forgotten empires beckon, and every stone might whisper a legend from the past. With deliberate care, he continued, "I offer you this chance not solely as a passenger, but as a potential keeper of tales—a companion who will help piece together the saga of our times."

As the soft light of dawn mingled with the murmurs of the departing night, the agreement was forged not with formal contracts but with the silent promises in two resolute eyes. John felt the stir of destiny as Pliny's hand rested on the fingerboard near the boat's helm—a subtle invitation to cross thresholds, both physical and metaphorical. In that moment, the vessel, its creaking planks and timeworn rigging resonating with history, became the threshold to a future filled with perilous wonders and stirring legends.

The promise of an extraordinary journey had been offered on the mystical shores of Patmos. With that first, measured handshake, John embarked on a path that would lead him far beyond the familiar journey where the ancient and the unknown intertwined, and where every tide held the potential to reveal secrets long thought lost.

The sun dipped low as Pliny's vessel approached the bustling harbor of Rhodes, painting the sky in a riot of molten golds and dusky purples. The tawny light stretched over ancient sandstone walls, each block etched with the scars and stories of centuries, glowing with an amber warmth that bordered on the otherworldly. As the boat cut through gentle ripples on the water, John could feel the cool, salt-tinged breeze brushing against his skin a tactile reminder of the vast, mysterious sea beyond.

Ships of every size bobbed in the harbor—a flotilla of sleek merchant vessels with shimmering masts, weathered fishing boats exuding the briny tang of the deep, and sturdy galleys that creaked with the weight of history. The air pulsed with life, filled with a medley of sounds: the low, rhythmic hum of rigging in the wind, the creak of wood against wood, and the lively banter of sailors exchanging tales of far-off lands. Overhead, gulls cried out piercing notes, their echoes blending seamlessly with the chatter of dockside tradesmen and the distant clamor of a jubilant marketplace.

The harbor was an aromatic tapestry. John inhaled deeply—the invigorating brine of the sea intermingled harmoniously with the earthy aroma of olive oil and the heady perfume of exotic spices. There was a peppery note of cumin and a hint of saffron that told tales of bazaars in distant lands. Every breath seemed to carry the weight of centuries, each scent a fragment of the cultural mosaic that Rhodes had become, a crossroads where the past and present collided.

As the boat glided closer to the quay, Pliny's calloused hand swept toward the horizon, his silhouette outlined by the lingering glow of twilight. "Look there," he murmured with reverence, his voice carrying the rasp of countless voyages. In the soft, low hum of the evening, John saw two stone pedestals guarding the entrance to the harbor. Their surfaces, worn smooth by centuries of relentless sea spray and the abrasions of biting winds, exuded an almost palpable nostalgia—a tangible relic of a bygone era when gods and men conversed in legends.

"They say it was the tallest thing ever built by human hands," Pliny continued, his tone laden with both reverence and melancholy. "A bronze giant, seventy cubits high, straddling the harbor with one mighty foot on each side—a marvel of its time, a beacon that welcomed weary sailors and bold merchants alike." John squinted into the vibrant dusk, picturing a colossal figure that once shone like polished metal under the sun's benevolent gaze, its very essence imbued with the hum of myth and magic. "What happened to it?"

he asked, his voice a mixture of curiosity and sorrow, as if yearning to touch the long-lost titan.

Pliny's laugh, harsh and brittle as broken pottery, resonated through the evening air. "The divine envy of the gods, or so the story goes. An earthquake—nature's relentless reminder of our fragility—brought it down over two hundred years ago. Its proud, shining pieces were scattered, sold off, melted down like so much spent treasure, leaving behind only whispers of what once was." The wind seemed to carry his words across the water, each syllable laden with the bitter tang of loss and the faint aroma of smoldering metal.

John nodded slowly, the image of the fallen giant mingling with his own sense of impermanence, a physical monument to the inevitable decay of human endeavors. Every sound around him—the creak of the dock, the clatter of hands unloading goods, and the distant murmur of lively conversations—filled him with both the vibrancy of life and the quiet echo of history slipping away.

The boat came to a gentle halt against the time-worn wooden planks of the dock, and Pliny moved with efficient grace, coiling ropes and securing the vessel as though every knot he tied was a safeguard against the ravages of time. The wood underfoot was rough and splintered in places, a tactile reminder of endless arrivals and departures, each board a silent witness to stories untold. The harbor itself was a living collage—a spectrum of colors from the scarlet and saffron awnings covering bustling market stalls, to the deep indigo of the evening sky merging with the sea.

"This is as far as I go," Pliny declared as he took a final lingering look at the vibrant scene around them. "You'll find someone here to continue your journey. Qumran is a long way yet, but Rhodes is the perfect starting point." As he spoke, his eyes shone with a blend of resignation and hope, echoing the age-old duality between the known and the unknown.

John met Pliny's gaze, the fading light catching the earnest determination within his eyes. "Thank you," he replied in a soft, measured tone, each syllable imbued with gratitude and a quiet, unspoken promise that he would honor the legacy of those who had come before him.

That night, Rhodes transformed under a veil of stars. John found refuge in a modest inn, its stone walls steeped in the murmur of distant legends and half-forgotten whispers of the past. The inn was cool and shadowed, its interior alive with the aromatic blend of woodsmoke and spiced wine. As he sat by the flickering candlelight, the soft crackle of the flame played a quiet symphony against the backdrop of the inn's murmuring corridors. Laying out a tattered map across a heavy oak table, John traced the sinuous, winding paths that led from the now ethereal grandeur of the harbor to the mysterious precincts of Qumran. Every drawn line felt like a heartbeat, pulsing with the possibility of undiscovered secrets and hidden realms.

During a humble supper of lentils and flatbread, served steaming on rustic ceramic plates, John listened intently as the innkeeper—a silver-haired sage with a voice that resonated like the chime of ancient bells—related the lore of Rhodes. "Every stone here has its own memory, every narrow alleyway hides a fragment of history," the old man said, his words rich with the warmth of human experience and the spice of distant lands. "They say even the gods wept when the Colossus fell. Now, its presence lingers in every shadow, every gust of wind that sweeps through our streets." The innkeeper's soft, melodic tones were interspersed with the gentle clinking of cutlery and hushed conversations, each sound amplifying the sense of mystery that pervaded the night.

Later, as John lay in a modest chamber with a small window framing the luminous night sky, he was assaulted by vivid dreams—a montage of sensory overload. In his sleep, the smell of crushed bronze, the haunting sound of a collapsing edifice, and the cold, hard sensation of shattered marble danced in unison. Each dream was a touch of the past, a tactile encounter with the legacy of the Colossus, leaving him with the bittersweet taste of memories that had long since faded from the annals of time.

At dawn, as the first feeble rays of sun painted the horizon in pastel hues of lavender and rose, the city of Rhodes awoke in a breathtaking display of life. John stepped out into the cool morning air, where the dewy mist clinging to ancient cobblestones mingled with the soft, lingering aroma of night-blooming jasmine. Wandering through narrow alleys, he was enveloped by the rich cacophony of daily life: the rhythmic clattering of footsteps on stone, the vibrant calls of vendors hawking their goods, and the occasional burst of laughter that seemed to echo off the centuries-old walls.

In a secluded courtyard bursting with greenery and dappled sunlight, John discovered a stunning mosaic—the interplay of blue and gold tiles capturing mythic scenes that stirred his soul. A local scholar known as Themistocles, with bright eyes as polished agate and a voice as smooth as well-aged wine, joined him. They shared a quiet moment beneath an ancient olive tree, its gnarled branches whispering secrets to the wind. Over cups of robust herbal tea that warmed his cold hands, Themistocles recounted tales interwoven with the scents of history and promise. "This island has witnessed empires rise and crumble," he said, his tone both proud and somber. "The Colossus was never merely a monument—it was our collective hope, our shared dream of a future unbound by time."

Every word resonated deeply, leaving John with the tactile impression of destiny pressed softly against his heart.

Yet even as the city flourished with its vibrant markets and lively conversations, an undercurrent tension simmered in subtle whispers and furtive glances. Beneath the bright clamor of commerce, the hardened pavement and shadowed doorways held flickers of a more somber reality a soft, relentless reminder that no era is immune to decay or strife. The sound of one's footsteps on ancient stone, intermingled with the murmur of clandestine discussions, added layers of complexity to Rhodes, inviting the observant traveler to trace the unseen scars of its storied past.

As dusk gradually draped its velvet cloak over the city once again, John found himself back at the harbor's edge. The stone pedestals, illuminated by the mellow glow of lanterns, stood like silent sentinels to a time of legends. The rhythmic lapping of waves against the dock and the distant hum of nocturnal life harmonized into a haunting lullaby—one that beckoned him to remember, to reflect, and ultimately, to commit himself to an odyssey that transcended the moment. In that suspended fragment of twilight, as the sensory details of night enveloped him, the cool rush of the breeze, the faint tang of salt in the air, and the bittersweet murmur of ancient tales—John vowed that his journey toward Qumran would be a pilgrimage of both discovery and remembrance.

Thus, with every sense alight and every moment saturated with the rich flavors of time and history, John resolved to step forward into the labyrinth of the past. The rhythmic pulse of Rhodes, its tactile textures and vivid sounds, would be his constant companion as he ventured into the corridors of legend—a quest to unearth the forgotten, to embrace the unknown, and to capture the ephemeral beauty of moments that, like the once-mighty Colossus, flickered brilliantly against the vast canvas of eternity. He would find passage to Qumran, he told himself. And when he did, the next step of his journey would begin.

Chapter Three
On to Qumran

Under a gentle blush of dawn on Patmos, Pliny's weathered vessel, its hull salt-crusted and time-honored, glided steadily toward the weathered quay. Unlike any boat John had ever flown his own colors on, this craft bore the unmistakable mark of its master—a testament to countless journeys and storied harbors. John, driven by a desire not merely to travel but to be part of something greater, had come to seek his passage: to secure a position on Pliny's crew and join him on the fabled voyage toward Rhodes.

Stepping off the gangway, John's keen eyes met those of the man whose life had been woven with the threads of adventure. Pliny stood near the vessel, his stance both commanding and weathered, as if the sea itself had sculpted his every line. In the soft morning air—tangled with the scent of brine, wild thyme, and the promise of discovery—John dared to introduce himself. "I have come seeking a chance to join a journey worth remembering," he said quietly, his tone imbued with both hope and humble determination.

Pliny's gaze, deep and searching as the ocean, flickered with a quiet acknowledgment. "Many have sought passage on this ship," he began, his voice low and measured, "but few possess both the spirit and resolve to bear witness to the mysteries that await beyond these familiar shores. Rhodes is no mere destination—it is a realm where the echoes of forgotten empires beckon, and every stone might whisper a legend from the past. With deliberate care, he continued, "I offer you this chance not solely as a passenger, but as a potential keeper of tales—a companion who will help piece together the saga of our times."

As the soft light of dawn mingled with the murmurs of the departing night, the agreement was forged not with formal contracts but with the silent promises in two resolute eyes. John felt the stir of destiny as Pliny's hand rested on the fingerboard near the boat's helm—a subtle invitation to cross thresholds, both physical and metaphorical. In that moment, the vessel, its creaking planks and timeworn rigging resonating with history, became the threshold to a future filled with perilous wonders and stirring legends.

The promise of an extraordinary journey had been offered on the mystical shores of Patmos. With that first, measured handshake, John embarked on a path that would lead him far beyond the familiar journey where the ancient and the unknown intertwined, and where every tide held the potential to reveal secrets long thought lost.

The sun dipped low as Pliny's vessel approached the bustling harbor of Rhodes, painting the sky in a riot of molten golds and dusky purples. The tawny light stretched over ancient sandstone walls, each block etched with the scars and stories of centuries, glowing with an amber warmth that bordered on the otherworldly. As the boat cut through gentle ripples on the water, John could feel the cool, salt-tinged breeze brushing against his skin a tactile reminder of the vast, mysterious sea beyond.

Ships of every size bobbed in the harbor—a flotilla of sleek merchant vessels with shimmering masts, weathered fishing boats exuding the briny tang of the deep, and sturdy galleys that creaked with the weight of history. The air pulsed with life, filled with a medley of sounds: the low, rhythmic hum of rigging in the wind, the creak of wood against wood, and the lively banter of sailors exchanging tales of far-off lands. Overhead, gulls cried out piercing notes, their echoes blending seamlessly with the chatter of dockside tradesmen and the distant clamor of a jubilant marketplace.

The harbor was an aromatic tapestry. John inhaled deeply—the invigorating brine of the sea intermingled harmoniously with the earthy aroma of olive oil and the heady perfume of exotic spices. There was a peppery note of cumin and a hint of saffron that told tales of bazaars in distant lands. Every breath seemed to carry the weight of centuries, each scent a fragment of the cultural mosaic that Rhodes had become, a crossroads where the past and present collided.

As the boat glided closer to the quay, Pliny's calloused hand swept toward the horizon, his silhouette outlined by the lingering glow of twilight. "Look there," he murmured with reverence, his voice carrying the rasp of countless voyages. In the soft, low hum of the evening, John saw two stone pedestals guarding the entrance to the harbor. Their surfaces, worn smooth by centuries of relentless sea spray and the abrasions of biting winds, exuded an almost palpable nostalgia—a tangible relic of a bygone era when gods and men conversed in legends.

"They say it was the tallest thing ever built by human hands," Pliny continued, his tone laden with both reverence and melancholy. "A bronze giant, seventy cubits high, straddling the harbor with one mighty foot on each side—a marvel of its time, a beacon that welcomed weary sailors and bold merchants alike." John squinted into the vibrant dusk, picturing a colossal figure that once shone like polished metal under the sun's benevolent gaze, its very essence imbued with the hum of myth and magic. "What happened to it?" he asked, his voice a mixture of curiosity and sorrow, as if yearning to touch the long-lost titan.

Pliny's laugh, harsh and brittle as broken pottery, resonated through the evening air. "The divine envy of the gods, or so the story goes. An earthquake—nature's relentless reminder of our fragility—brought it down over two hundred years ago. Its proud, shining pieces were scattered, sold off, melted down like so much spent treasure, leaving behind only whispers of what once was." The wind seemed to carry his words across the water, each syllable laden with the bitter tang of loss and the faint aroma of smoldering metal.

John nodded slowly, the image of the fallen giant mingling with his own sense of impermanence, a physical monument to the inevitable decay of human endeavors. Every sound around him—the creak of the dock, the clatter of hands unloading goods, and the distant murmur of lively conversations—filled him with both the vibrancy of life and the quiet echo of history slipping away.

The boat came to a gentle halt against the time-worn wooden planks of the dock, and Pliny moved with efficient grace, coiling ropes and securing the vessel as though every knot he tied was a safeguard against the ravages of time. The wood underfoot was rough and splintered in places, a tactile reminder of endless arrivals and departures, each board a silent witness to stories untold. The harbor itself was a living collage—a spectrum of colors from the scarlet and saffron awnings covering bustling market stalls, to the deep indigo of the evening sky merging with the sea.

"This is as far as I go," Pliny declared as he took a final lingering look at the vibrant scene around them. "You'll find someone here to continue your journey. Qumran is a long way yet, but Rhodes is the perfect starting point." As he spoke, his eyes shone with a blend of resignation and hope, echoing the age-old duality between the known and the unknown.

John met Pliny's gaze, the fading light catching the earnest determination within his eyes. "Thank you," he replied in a soft, measured tone, each syllable imbued with gratitude and a quiet, unspoken promise that he would honor the legacy of those who had come before him.

That night, Rhodes transformed under a veil of stars. John found refuge in a modest inn, its stone walls steeped in the murmur of distant legends and half-forgotten whispers of the past. The inn was cool and shadowed, its interior alive with the aromatic blend of woodsmoke and spiced wine. As he sat by the flickering candlelight, the soft crackle of the flame played a quiet symphony against the backdrop of the inn's murmuring corridors. Laying out a tattered map across a heavy oak table, John traced the sinuous, winding paths that led from the now ethereal grandeur of the harbor to the mysterious precincts of Qumran. Every drawn line felt like a heartbeat, pulsing with the possibility of undiscovered secrets and hidden realms.

During a humble supper of lentils and flatbread, served steaming on rustic ceramic plates, John listened intently as the innkeeper—a silver-haired sage with a voice that resonated like the chime of ancient bells—related the lore of Rhodes. "Every stone here has its own memory, every narrow alleyway hides a fragment of history," the old man said, his words rich with the warmth of human experience and the spice of distant lands. "They say even the gods wept when the Colossus fell. Now, its presence lingers in every shadow, every gust of wind that sweeps through our streets." The innkeeper's soft, melodic tones were interspersed with the gentle clinking of cutlery and hushed conversations, each sound amplifying the sense of mystery that pervaded the night.

Later, as John lay in a modest chamber with a small window framing the luminous night sky, he was assaulted by vivid dreams—a montage of sensory overload. In his sleep, the smell of crushed bronze, the haunting sound of a collapsing edifice, and the cold, hard sensation of shattered marble danced in unison. Each dream was a touch of the past, a tactile encounter with the legacy of the Colossus, leaving him with the bittersweet taste of memories that had long since faded from the annals of time.

At dawn, as the first feeble rays of sun painted the horizon in pastel hues of lavender and rose, the city of Rhodes awoke in a breathtaking display of life. John stepped out into the cool morning air, where the dewy mist clinging to ancient cobblestones mingled with the soft, lingering aroma of night-blooming jasmine. Wandering through narrow alleys, he was enveloped by the rich cacophony of daily life: the rhythmic clattering of footsteps on stone, the vibrant calls of vendors hawking their goods, and the occasional burst of laughter that seemed to echo off the centuries-old walls.

In a secluded courtyard bursting with greenery and dappled sunlight, John discovered a stunning mosaic—the interplay of blue and gold tiles capturing mythic scenes that stirred his soul. A local scholar known as Themistocles, with bright eyes as polished agate and a voice as smooth as well-aged wine, joined him. They shared a quiet moment beneath an ancient olive tree, its gnarled branches whispering secrets to the wind. Over cups of robust herbal tea that warmed his cold hands, Themistocles recounted tales interwoven with the scents of history and promise. "This island has witnessed empires rise and crumble," he said, his tone both proud and somber. "The Colossus was never merely a monument—it was our collective hope, our shared dream of a future unbound by time."

Every word resonated deeply, leaving John with the tactile impression of destiny pressed softly against his heart.

Yet even as the city flourished with its vibrant markets and lively conversations, an undercurrent tension simmered in subtle whispers and furtive glances. Beneath the bright clamor of commerce, the hardened pavement and shadowed doorways held flickers of a more somber reality a soft, relentless reminder that no era is immune to decay or strife. The sound of one's footsteps on ancient stone, intermingled with the murmur of clandestine discussions, added layers of complexity to Rhodes, inviting the observant traveler to trace the unseen scars of its storied past.

As dusk gradually draped its velvet cloak over the city once again, John found himself back at the harbor's edge. The stone pedestals, illuminated by the mellow glow of lanterns, stood like silent sentinels to a time of legends. The rhythmic lapping of waves against the dock and the distant hum of nocturnal life harmonized into a haunting lullaby—one that beckoned him to remember, to reflect, and ultimately, to commit himself to an odyssey that transcended the moment. In that suspended fragment of twilight, as the sensory details of night enveloped him, the cool rush of the breeze, the faint tang of salt in the air, and the bittersweet murmur of ancient tales—John vowed that his journey toward Qumran would be a pilgrimage of both discovery and remembrance.

Thus, with every sense alight and every moment saturated with the rich flavors of time and history, John resolved to step forward into the labyrinth of the past. The rhythmic pulse of Rhodes, its tactile textures and vivid sounds, would be his constant companion as he ventured into the corridors of legend—a quest to unearth the forgotten, to embrace the unknown, and to capture the ephemeral beauty of moments that, like the once-mighty Colossus, flickered brilliantly against the vast canvas of eternity. He would find passage to Qumran, he told himself. And when he did, the next step of his journey would begin.

Chapter Four
The Meeting

Qumran stood as a lone bastion against the encroaching chaos of the outside world. Nestled between the harsh, sun-beaten expanse of the Judean Desert and the shimmering, enigmatic waters of the Dead Sea, the settlement exuded almost other worldly majesty. Its ancient walls and austere cisterns bore silent testimony to countless generations who had sought refuge from corruption and strife. Here, the Essenes did not simply dwell—they forged a spiritual bulwark. To them, Qumran was a sanctified battleground, a retreat where the Sons of Light braced themselves for the inevitable clash with the Sons of Darkness, as foretold in the sacred War Rule.

The air itself was heavy with portent; the rhythmic hiss of wind over stone was intermingled with the ancient scent of salt and the faint, lingering aroma of burning incense. Ingeniously constructed aqueducts wound their way through the settlement like silver threads, channeling life-sustaining water to vast underground cisterns. Every stone laid in Qumran's formidable walls seemed imbued with purpose, placed not by accident but by hands driven by unwavering faith and divine conviction. In the quiet hours before dusk, intangible chants rose in soft, measured cadence—a shared prayer that blurred the lines between ritual and revelation.

Beyond the settlement's boundaries, the cliffs stood sentinel, their faces etched with the erosion of countless years. Hidden within these natural ramparts lay a network of caves, each guard to secrets both mundane and miraculous. Some caverns sheltered sacred scrolls, safeguarded meticulously from the ruthless corruption of Roman dominion; others served as chambers of silent meditation and divine communion. The most revered of these were the vaults which enshrined the War Rule—the apocalyptic scripture that detailed the ceaseless struggle between ephemeral light and the encroaching darkness. For the Essenes, the War Rule was both prophecy and strategy; its austere verses served as a divine blueprint for the battles of spirit and sinew that lay ahead.

High above the settlement, Eleazar—the ever-vigilant sentry—stood perched upon the ancient cliffs. His silhouette, stark against the deepening hues of twilight, was fixed in concentration as his keen eyes scanned the desolate horizon. It was near sundown, in that precarious hour when the day yields to the mysteries of night, that Eleazar first noticed the solitary figure making its way along the inlet. The figure's gait was deliberate, the cloak swirling about him in the whispering desert wind. Eleazar's brow furrowed with suspicion, for strangers rarely trod the well-guarded paths of Qumran. History had taught them that unknown visitors could be harbingers of either revelation or ruin.

Without delay, Eleazar descended into the heart of Qumran, joining the council of elders gathered in a chamber lit only by the wavering glow of oil lamps. The central chamber, carved deep into the living rock, was a study in shadows and hushed tension. At its center sat Abiram, the chief elder, whose lined face bore both the wisdom and weariness of decades spent in the service of providence. At his side, Hoshiah—the devoted keeper of the sacred texts—cradled an ancient parchment inscribed with solemn lines from the War Rule, while Baraqiel, guardian of the labyrinthine caves, lingered near the entrance like a silent sentinel.

"There is a man approaching the cliffs," Eleazar announced in a voice as measured as the turning hour. "He walks alone, yet his bearing speaks of purpose. Strangers bring neither comfort nor assurance here—unless they come bearing the truth or the chaos of unbidden revelation." Abiram's eyes, deep and knowing, exchanged silent communication with Hoshiah. "Purpose," Abiram intoned, "can be a guise for ruination. Ruin often arrives unbidden, cloaked in the semblance of destiny. We must proceed with caution." At that

THE MEETING

moment, Baraqiel stepped forward. "The War Rule warns us of deception," he reminded them gravely. "A visitor may carry wisdom, yet he might also bear falsehood. We must test his intent."

With agreement resonating around him, Abiram commanded, "Send Azariah." The emissary descended swiftly—a young man whose quiet grace belied the intensity glimmering in his dark eyes and whose carefully chosen words were tempered by both respect and a relentless curiosity. Under the ghostly illumination of the moon, Azariah met the approaching stranger at the frosted base of the cliffs.

A brittle silence stretched between them until Azariah finally spoke. "You stand at the threshold of Qumran," he said in a measured tone that blended welcome with wary inquiry. "Speak, stranger. What brings you to our sacred refuge?" The visitor, whose tired eyes mirrored long journeys and inner battles, lifted his gaze with reluctant resolve. "Visions have summoned me here," he replied, his voice trembling between certainty and desperation. When pressed for details, he admitted softly, "I have seen fire and shadow—a collapse and a renewal, all interwoven in a tapestry of both ruin and rebirth."

Azariah's gaze narrowed as he digested these cryptic revelations. "The War Rule speaks of tumultuous end-times—a struggle betwixt light and darkness," he murmured. "Yet many claim visions of conflagration and gloom, and only the true bearer of destiny may discern their meaning. Come with me; you shall stand before the council and reveal your purpose, for it is they who shall determine the path that awaits you." And so, beneath the watchful eyes of ancient stones imbued with secret lore, Azariah led the enigmatic traveler toward the core of Qumran.

Inside the settlement, every stone and ritual pulsed with sacred significance. Along narrow, time-worn passageways, the Essenes moved with deliberate purpose. Keziah, the meticulous archivist, arranged fragile scrolls with a reverence born of generations dedicated to divine study. Shalem, the dedicated astronomer, climbed a modest platform to chart the celestial dance of stars and planets—each cosmic movement interpreted as a divine sign nested within the verses of the War Rule. Tzefaniah, the alchemist of herbs and healing, ground fragrant botanicals, transforming them into mixtures intended to fortify both body and spirit. Jedidiah, ever the steadfast watchman, patrolled the perimeter with his carved staff—a living embodiment of vigilance. Even Adinah, the weaver, labored quietly at her loom, crafting garments of pristine white that symbolized the purity and promise of the faithful.

Every action, every whispered prayer, every gesture was dictated by the eternal precepts of the War Rule. Its austere declarations were recited in moments of solitude and crisis alike, a constant reminder that the battle between divine illumination and encroaching darkness was not one of distant myth, but a present and pervasive reality. It was against this backdrop of unwavering faith and steely resolve that John—the seeker of visions—was escorted to the inner sanctum of Qumran.

In a chamber carved from ancient bedrock and bathed in the flickering light of oil lamps, Abiram awaited him. The air was redolent with the scent of herbs smoldered in ritual, and the flickering shadows on the walls seemed to pulse with the heartbeat of destiny. Abiram's piercing gaze fell upon John as he stepped forward, the tension in the room palpable, laden with the unspoken promise of trials to come. "You come bearing visions of the end," Abiram declared, his voice resonant with authority borne of countless hardships. "But remember: the end is not solely a harbinger of your destruction—it is the reclamation of light, the ushering in of divine will. The War Rule has taught us that annihilation is only the precursor to transformation."

John's voice wavered as he responded, "My visions are of fire and shadow, yes—but they also speak of a beginning, a hidden truth that lies dormant within these halls and among these cliffs. I believe that something vital here holds the key to what must be done." Abiram's gaze deepened, as if peering into realms unseen. "Many come seeking keys," he said slowly, "but few understand the nature of the locks they must open. Should your purpose prove true, Qumran will unveil its mysteries to you. But if your claim is false... beware the wrath that the divine commands."

As the elders murmured among themselves, an oppressive silence laid its claim over the chamber. In that charged moment, John felt the cumulative weight of centuries of belief and expectation press against him, a crushing reminder that his path was irrevocably intertwined with both peril and promise. Abiram stood, his movements deliberate and measured, and pronounced, "Tomorrow you shall be tested. When the light of dawn reveals all, you must confront the truth of your visions." With those ominous words suspended in the dim air, the council retreated into the shadows, leaving John to the swirling echoes of fate.

That night, Qumran transformed into a realm of hushed incantations and secret reflections. In the labyrinthine corridors of stone, John wandered alone, each step resonating on the ancient flagstones. The silence was broken only by the soft susurration of distant prayers and the rhythmic drip of water from the miraculous aqueducts. In the solitude of these sacred halls, his mind replayed the stark images of his visions: conflagrations dancing with phantom shadows, and luminous flashes of rebirth emerging from desolation. Was his arrival here a matter of divine destiny, or a cruel twist of fate? The questions, like the chamber's wavering shadows, held little answer but echoed in the recesses of his soul.

Outside, the desert night stretched unyielding and vast. The relentless wind carried with it the whispers of ancient lore, swirling around the olive trees and over the arid crags. In one quiet moment, John paused beneath an archway that opened to the endless dark threshold between mortal frailty and the eternal mysteries inscribed in the War Rule. There, the delicate murmur of the desert spoke to him as though it was a long-forgotten hymn, urging him onward even as fear coiled in his heart. He could almost sense the presence of those who had come before—a tapestry of voices from eras past—reminding him that every soul in Qumran had, at one time, stood at the precipice of destiny.

Not long after, Azariah returned to John's side. His voice, soft and imbued with quiet gravity, broke the spell of isolation. "The trial you are to face is not one of mere physical endurance," he confided. "Deep within the caverns beneath our sanctuary lie challenges of spirit and will. Only those who confront both their inner darkness and the harsh brilliance of truth emerge enlightened." John listened intently to the solemnity of Azariah's words mingling with the residual echoes of his own visions. "I feel the pull," John admitted in a low tone, "as if every step I have taken has led me to this very moment—my purpose interlaced with the fate of you all and the ever-present dichotomy of light and shadow."

As the hours before dawn dwindled, Qumran itself seemed to awaken in quiet expectancy. In one of the dimly lit study chambers, Hoshiah delicately unfurled ancient scrolls and began transcribing fervent interpretations of the War Rule. His ink-stained fingers moved reverently over the timeworn parchment, each stroking a silent prayer for clarity in a world fraught with omens. The voices of the elders, the fervor of the faithful, and the whispered prophecies contained within those sacred texts converged in the stillness of that long, watchful night.

Outside, the first hints of dawn crept over the horizon, tinting the sky with fragile streaks of amber and silver. In the central courtyard, the Essenes gathered in quiet contemplation. Their voices, low and resonant, rose in a subdued litany—a harmonious blend of prayer and vigilance that reasserted their steadfast belief in the ultimate triumph of divine light. The gathering was a living mosaic of hope and resolve, each soul acutely aware of the stakes at hand, for they had long known that the flame of hope flickered brightest in the harshest darkness.

John's restless mind was finally granted a fleeting reprieve as he found himself drawn to one of the ancient cisterns. Tracing his fingers along the worn inscriptions on the cool stone, he felt as if the very essence of Qumran were speaking to him—a silent assurance that his trial was not a curse but an invitation to a profound transformation. Each droplet of water that trickled along the channel seemed to echo the combined prayers of generations, urging him to embrace the impending test not as a mark of doom, but as a visionary passage into a new beginning.

As the sun ascended, dispelling the fragile shadows of night, a palpable shift rippled through Qumran. The community, ever vigilant yet emboldened by the revelations of the past hours, braced itself for the day ahead a day in which the visions of fire and shadow would be scrutinized, and the true mettle of faith measured against the divine scales of destiny. Standing on the threshold of this pivotal moment, John felt the weight of his journey converge with the unyielding resolve of the Essenes. It was here, between the ancient stones and eternal sands, that the eternal struggle between light and darkness would once again be a waged struggle that would define not only his fate but also the legacy of a people who had dedicated their lives to guarding the sanctity of truth.

In the final, charged moments before the trial was to commence, as the desert's warm light mingled with the lingering chill of prophetic night, John could sense that everything was poised on the edge of transformation. The echoes of the War Rule stirred in every whispered prayer, every meticulous inscription, and every brave heartbeat. The forthcoming test, shrouded in both promise and peril, would reveal whether the visions burning within him were the heralds of illumination or omens of despair. And in that transcendent interval, beneath the unwavering watch of ancient cliffs and the steadfast eyes of the faithful, the souls of Qumran prepared to witness the dawning of a new chapter one where destiny and divine purpose would ultimately intertwine.

Thus, as the morning sunbathed the sacred settlement in a resolute glow, Qumran stood ready a living emblem of hope and defiance. Its stones whispered of past glories and future triumphs, of battles waged in both physical and spiritual realms. And as John braced himself for the coming trial, the eternal cadence of the desert and the sacred verses of the War Rule wove together into an inexorable call—a call to confront darkness, embrace light, and, in the crucible of destiny, discover the true strength of the human spirit.

Chapter Five
The Chamber of Whispers

The chamber in Qumran was a place of solemn reverence, a sanctuary carved from ancient stone and weathered by centuries of fervent prayer and lingering prophecy. Its walls, rough and scarred by the steady passage of time, held the echoes of hushed conversations and heartfelt supplications. Every crevice and fissure seemed to pulse with the voices of countless souls long past, their secrets mingling with the soft rustle of worn parchments stored on carved shelves. The flickering light of oil lamps cast shifting shadows that danced across the stone, creating phantasmal silhouettes that made it seem as though the very walls breathed with a life of their own.

In the center of the vast, low-ceilinged room, John stood alone. The cool, uneven surface of the stone floor underfoot grounded him in the present, yet his heart pounded as if in anticipation of another heartbeat. His body was weary from endless nights of travel, and his mind, frayed by restless visions, was a maelstrom of half-heard voices and shimmering images. Yet, his spirit remained drawn taut like a bowstring—ready to launch into the unknown even as the echoes of his past pressed on him like the bittersweet taste of ancient wine.

Around him, the elders bided their time in a near silence charged with anxiety. Their eyes—sharp and unyielding—assessed him with a mix of suspicion and unspoken dread. At the helm of the council sat Abiram, whose presence dominated the dim space. He looked every inch the spectral arbiter of fate, his flowing robes moving as if propelled by an unseen force. His steely gaze bore into John, as if trying to unravel the secrets hidden in the lines of his worn face—the same way one might size up a serpent secretly coiled within the folds of a heavy cloak: dangerous, unpredictable, and yet potentially revelatory.

Breaking the heavy pause, Abiram's gravelly voice rolled through the chamber like distant thunder.

"You have claimed visions of the end," he intoned, his tone resonant with the weight of prophecy. "You bring claims of purpose and of impending peril. Yet we do not know you. Step forward now and speak your truth."

John's heart hammered in his ears as he took a hesitant step forward. Each footfall echoed on the cold stone, mingling with the soft, almost imperceptible drip of moisture falling from the high, vaulted ceiling. His dry lips struggled to shape the words that had haunted him since that fateful night on Patmos—a memory as haunting as the wail of a mournful wind. The cool draft carrying a faint trace of incense and desert dust tugged at him as if urging him to reveal his tale.

"My name is John of Patmos," he finally declared, his words breaking through the hush like ripples across a still pond. The declaration, simple yet profound, seemed to stir the very air around him. A ripple of murmurs spread like wildfire among the elders.

Hoshiah, the devoted keeper of sacred texts, stiffened visibly. His ink-stained fingers gripped a fragile parchment as though their trembling could somehow anchor him to the certainty of the past.

"John of Patmos," he whispered, the reverence in his hushed tone mingling with the scent of worn parchment and the faint, lingering smoke of incense. "Exiled by Nero himself. It is said you were cast to die on that forsaken isle."

John's eyes, shadowed by grief and hardened resolve, met Hoshiah's trembling gaze. "Yes. Nero declared me an enemy and abandoned me to rot amidst the barren winds. But the isle—its isolation became not my doom, but my crucible of revelation."

A sharp intake of breath from Baraqiel, whose tone cut through the tension like a brittle whisper, soon followed. "And yet you live," he observed, the underlying suspicion thick in his voice. "What sustained you? What force allowed you to survive such desolation?"

For a long, weighted moment, John's throat constricted as memories surged back of dark, damp caves and nights spent shivering in eerie solitude. "The visions," he managed in a strained voice that cracked under the burden of remembrance. "They showed me things I cannot unsee. They kept me awake in the silence of despair—they kept me alive. And they revealed the Beast."

At the utterance of that single word—Beast—a palpable chill descended upon the chamber, as though the temperature itself had dropped inside an ancient vault. Even Tzefaniah, renowned for her unflappable calm, shifted uncomfortably. Her slender fingers fidgeted at the hem of her robe, and the flickering lamps seemed to dim, their warm glow swallowed by a sudden, oppressive shadow.

Abiram's deep-set eyes narrowed as he demanded, "You speak of the Beast. Explain."

John drew a deep, shuddering breath, his hands trembling as he reached out into the charged air before him, as if attempting to grasp the intangible shapes of his haunted memories. "It is Nero," he began, his voice growing heavy with the gravity of his revelation. "Or perhaps it is more than Nero—a force beyond mortal reckoning, harnessing him as its vessel." His pause was laden with the sound of his racing heart echoing in his ears before he continued, "I saw the mark—the number. It is 666."

A collective gasp swept through the chamber, soft and chilling as the distant howl of wind over a barren desert at midnight. John's narrative gathered pace despite his internal tremors. "Neron Kaisar—Nero Caesar—it is encoded in the letters. ,☐☐☐☐ ☐☐☐written in Hebrew, sings the truth of the mark of the Beast. The digits, perfectly aligned, carry a curse inscribed in time."

As he spoke, the shadows on the stone walls were writhed and twisted, as if animated by his words. In that moment, John thought he heard faint, spectral murmurs—voices from his visions mingling with the ancient chants of prayer that the elders had long memorized.

Hoshiah's voice, barely more than a whisper amid the heavy silence, inquired, "And what did this Beast do?"

John's gaze darkened like storm clouds gathering over a desolate sea. His tone dropped to a shambling, eerie whisper, "It emerged from the depths of the darkened waters—a monstrous aberration, a blasphemy against the order of creation. Its form was a nightmarish blend of beasts: horns that curved like crescent moons, claws that glinted with the cold gleam of death, and scales that shimmered in an unnatural, sickly hue. Following in its wake were legions of shadows—the Sons of Darkness—whose agonized cries blended with the clamor of dying cities."

He paused, as if the very air around him grew thick with his recollection. "The earth burned beneath its fury; its surface splitting open to unleash rivers of molten fire that devoured entire civilizations. The skies churned with a violent tempest of flame and smoke, smothering the sun, while the stars themselves cascaded like falling embers into an abyss of endless night. I witnessed temples crumble into dust and rivers run red with the blood of the innocent, all beneath the malevolent, cruel laughter of the Beast—a laughter that echoed like broken glass in the silent void."

Every word that left John's lips felt like a tremor ripping the long-held stillness of the chamber. His own hands clenched into tight fists, as if trying to hold back the torrent of horror swirling within his mind. The elders sat motionless, their faces ghostly pale in the wavering lamplight; even Abiram's knuckles were white as he gripped the worn armrest of his stone throne, his expression a mask of contemplative dread.

Yet John's revelations did not end with ruin. His voice, though still quivering with raw emotion, began a quieter, almost hypnotic cadence. "And in the midst of that all-consuming darkness," he confessed, "I saw a light—a piercing, radiant light that came from the heavens and shattered the void. From that brilliance emerged the Sons of Light, clad in armor that shimmered as if forged by the divine. They marched unyieldingly toward the looming shadow, their righteous weapons gleaming in the fire's reflection. I saw the elemental clash: fire meeting fire, shadow meeting light—a battle so fierce that it seemed the fate of all creation hung by a single, slender thread."

The chamber itself appeared to breathe alongside his words. The elders shifted uneasily, the interplay of shadows and light across the walls echoing the tumult of emotions. Tzefaniah, her normally assured voice disrupted by tremors of both fear and hope, murmured, "The War Rule foretells such a battle. Its words, however, are not meant solely for mortal hearts. To witness what you have seen is both a divine blessing and a terrible curse."

Abiram finally broke the thick silence. "And you believe that the key to this looming battle lies hidden within these sacred walls?" he asked, his tone measured yet edged with unyielding authority.

John's eyes blazed with a fervor born of desperation and conviction. "Yes, with every heartbeat that has brought me here, my visions have led me to Qumran. There is something concealed here—something interwoven with the scrolls, perhaps hidden within the secretive recesses of the caves—that holds the power to prepare us for what must soon come."

For a long, heavy moment, Abiram regarded John as peering deep into the labyrinth of his soul, searching for both truth and treachery. Slowly, with a deliberate grace, he rose. "Truth is often obscured by inky shadows," he pronounced, his voice echoing off the ancient stone. "Yet I detect no deceit within your words. Your visions, as harrowing as they are, align too closely with the sacred lore we have guarded for generations. The Sons of Light shall lend you aid, John of Patmos. Together, we will uncover that which lies hidden and ready ourselves for the coming strife."

A faint murmur of assent whispered through the gathered elders, though an undercurrent of foreboding still clung to the air like desert dust in a weary breeze. As John bowed his head in solemn relief, he could not shake the sensation that the shadows had deepened—growing darker and more oppressive. The whispers in his mind, previously mere echoes, now swelled with an urgency that threatened to drown him in memory and dread.

One by one, the elders began to disperse into the labyrinth of quiet corridors and stone passageways, their measured steps echoing like distant drumbeats on a journey toward destiny. Abiram lingered at his place, eyes unfocused as if gazing beyond the tangible realm into some obscure, preordained future. John, his own attention caught by the irregular play of light from the oil lamps—each flicker dancing along the rough-hewn surfaces like a spectral warning—watched in silent contemplation.

Outside, far beyond the heavy oak door of the chamber, the desert night howled softly. The chilly wind scrambled its way through narrow alleys and around the ancient walls of Qumran, carrying with it the distant sounds of stone rubbing against stone, and whispers that merged with the mournful sigh of the landscape. It was as if the entire world, from the smallest shard of sand to the towering cliffs overhead, was holding its breath in anticipation of the judgment that lay ahead.

John's mind, still reeling from the cascade of revelations, found no peace. Though the trial had ended, the harrowing specter of the Beast—its laughter echoing like a ghostly refrain—remained etched within him. Every flicker of light and every sigh of the wind resonated with the memory of that cruel, haunting sound. As he lingered in the solitude of the chamber, his senses caught every detail: the acrid tang of burning incense mixed with the earthy scent of ancient stone, the cool, damp caress of the night's air on his skin, and the distant murmur of voices both human and spectral.

Outside, the desert and the night remained in a state of quiet rebellion, their inky darkness promising more trials yet. And as John prepared himself to step into the unknown—knowing deep in his bones that his journey was just beginning—he felt the inescapable pulse of destiny thrumming through every fiber of his being. With every breath drawn amidst the whispers of prophecy, he embraced both the weight of his past and the blazing uncertainty of the future.

Chapter Six
Dawn of Reckoning

The first light of morning broke over the Judean cliffs, the sky streaked with resplendent hues of gold and rose. The desert, vast and ancient, awakened to the soft caress of cool air, a temporary reprieve before the ruthless, searing heat of day took hold. Each grain of sand seemed to shimmer in the nascent light, and the craggy cliffs glowed as if dusted with celestial fire. The sound of a distant breeze—whispering like ancient spirits over the rocky outcroppings—mixed with the muted calls of desert birds beginning their day.

Within the fortified walls of Qumran, the Essenes gathered in their time-worn council chamber. This room, carved out of living rock and steeped in years of prayer and prophecy, spoke to the ages. The chamber's stone floor, cool and uneven under bare feet, vibrated gently with the murmur of hushed anticipation. Oil lamps, their flames wavering in the subtle morning draft, cast shifting shadows that danced against rough-hewn walls. The interplay of light and dark created a tapestry of moving silhouettes that seemed to breathe with the heartbeat of the community. In the air hung the mixed scents of fragrant incense, ancient parchment, and the faint tang of mineral-rich stone—all underscored by a lingering note of desert dew.

At the center of the chamber, the elders sat around a massive, time-scarred stone table, each face etched with lines of both sorrow and determination. Abiram, the chief elder, rose as though summoned by destiny. His deep-set eyes glowed with the gravity of impending choices, and his voice, when he spoke, carried the somber timbre of prophetic warning.

"We have heard the visions of John of Patmos," Abiram intoned, his words reverberating softly off the stone walls, "and we know the darkness that rises in Rome. Nero, the Beast, moves against all that is sacred. To ignore this is to invite annihilation."

As his resonant voice faded into the gentle clatter of the council's shifting, Hoshiah—the keeper of the sacred texts—leaned forward, his weathered hands curled around a fragile scroll. The smell of ink and aged parchment mingled with the mustiness of the chamber, and his voice, tinged with skeptical caution, broke the charged silence.

"We are a people of the scrolls and the spirit, not soldiers. What can we do against the Beast when his reach spans the world?"

The tone of Hoshiah's words was cool and measured, like a soft breeze before a gathering storm, yet his eyes betrayed an inner doubt that rippled beneath his calm exterior.

Tzefaniah, the healer whose presence invoked both comfort and quiet resolve, interjected with a voice as gentle as a lullaby yet firm as the bedrock beneath their feet. Her hands, clad in worn linen, moved expressively as she spoke.

"Even a small flame can light the way in the darkness, Hoshiah. Perhaps what John speaks of—the Ark—can become that flame. It is our spark against the coming night."

For a long moment, the gathered Essenes absorbed the weight of her suggestion, the delicate aroma of freshly ground herbs from her satchel mingling with the incense as if to sanctify her words.

All eyes gradually turned to John, who had maintained a cautious silence until now. His presence, weathered by hardship yet glowing with otherworldly intensity, commanded the room. Slowly, as if compelled by both dread and determination, John stepped forward into the pool of soft morning light streaming through a narrow, arched window. Each step echoed against the stone floor, a reminder of the journey he had endured—from the desolation of Patmos to the sacred refuge of Qumran. His throat felt parched, as if the blazing desert itself had scorched his voice, yet he found the strength to speak.

"The Ark of the Covenant is no mere relic," he began, his voice resonating with the quiet assurance of someone who has seen both ruin and redemption. "It is a vessel of divine power—an emissary of hope that can empower the Sons of Light to stand against the encroaching darkness."

A ripple of murmurs spread through the council like a delicate harp string vibrating in the early breeze. Abiram's eyes widened for an instant, as if the very words John uttered illuminated hidden shadows. With a raised hand, he restored order.

"If the Ark is indeed our weapon against Nero," Abiram said slowly, each word measured and heavy, "then where is it? And how are we to reclaim it from the clutches of forgotten time?"

A murmur of dissent and concern gripped the room as Baraqiel, the grave and thoughtful guardian of the caves, straightened his posture. The faint scent of damp earth and ancient stone clung to him as he set his words carefully.

"The Ark was hidden away to protect it from the corrupting touch of the unworthy. Our records, preserved through countless trials, whisper that it lies near Elephantine Island—ensconced within the embrace of the mighty Nile."

A stunned silence fell. In that quiet, even the soft crackle of an oil lamp seemed to hold its breath. Keziah, the archivist, her eyes alight with both hope and trepidation, spoke next in a hushed tone that vibrated with urgency.

"Elephantine Island—a place once graced by our people. But it is distant, and the peril of that journey is grave. Should Nero's agents become aware of our plans, they would strike without hesitation."

Abiram pressed his hand firmly on the stone table, the rough surface grounding his resolve.

"We must proceed with precision. This is not a mission to be rushed or taken lightly. Every step must be shrouded in secrecy and strategy."

The discussion deepened as morning advanced. Shalem, the astronomer whose eyes constantly sought wisdom in the heavens, unfurled a rough map on a piece of weathered parchment. His ink, dark and purposeful, danced across the paper as he detailed the route toward Elephantine, his fingers leaving faint traces of charcoal on the surface. With a muted flourish, he explained:

"Elephantine lies far to the south, nestled within the Nile's vast labyrinth. Our path will intersect with Roman checkpoints, and we must travel as shadows—unseen and unheard."

Nethaniah, the waterkeeper, who had spent countless hours tending to cool, crystal streams that hinted at ancient life beneath the arid land, leaned over the map. His furrowed brow and the taste of river salt upon his lips gave weight to his question:

"The Nile itself is fraught with dangers. With Roman warships prowling its changing currents, how do we ensure safe passage without drawing unwanted attention?"

Baraqiel stroked his thick beard thoughtfully as if recalling old secret meetings and brokered alliances.

"We have covert allies—a network of operatives embedded in Egypt's bustling trade. They walk among the merchants, unseen yet ever watchful. It is through these trusted hands that we must find our path."

John's voice grew stronger as he stepped forward once more, his eyes reflective pools of determination and sorrow.

"And what of Rome? If the Ark is to become our weapon in the final reckoning, it cannot remain hidden in the remote corners of a forgotten isle. It must be reclaimed and brought to the very heart of Nero's dominion."

At this, Abiram's deep gaze shifted towards the mosaic of faces gathered in the chamber.

"Indeed. Our allies within Rome must be alerted as well. This cannot end with the Ark alone—it is but the spark that will ignite the larger uprising against the Beast's tyranny."

The conversation soon turned to the labyrinthine intrigues that wove through Rome like poison in the city's ancient veins. Even Elior, the pragmatic cook—whose gruff exterior belied a wisdom born from life on the margins—voiced a concern in a low, measured tone:

"Rome is a city of veiled whispers and shifting allegiances. Every shadow conceals an enemy, and every step must be taken in absolute stealth. We risk exposure at every turn."

Tzefaniah responded, her calm resolve mixing with an ever-present warmth, as if channeling the healing essence of a sacred spring:

"That is why our operation will not stand alone, but in concert with those who despise Nero's cruelty. We have sympathizers even within the Senate—those who yearn for a new dawn free from tyranny. Our message will reach them, veiled in code so that even if intercepted, it reveals nothing of our true intent."

Keziah, ever the meticulous archivist, interwove her own affirmation with a sharp undercurrent of determination, the aroma of freshly unrolled scrolls filling the space:

"Our communications must be as subtle as the shifting sands. Coded messages, hidden symbols, every word a double entendre. If Nero catches wind of even a fragment of our design, we are finished before we begin."

Shalem tapped his quill against the map again—its tip leaving faint impressions on the parchment—as he plaintively offered another piece of the puzzle:

> "Then our envoy to Rome must be one of trust—a soul who knows that city's perilous rhythm, its splendor mingled with lurking shadows. Only then can our communication pierce the veil of Roman surveillance."

All eyes turned back to John, the solitary bearer of visions. The weight of expectation, like a tangible force, pressed upon him. Abiram's gaze, filled with both hope and the mourning of countless past sacrifices, met his.

> "You, John of Patmos, have seen the end that fate may bring—and the path that could redeem us. Should we reclaim the Ark, will you travel to Rome, to carry our message of rebellion and hope?"

John's pause stretched, each second heavy with the taste of destiny and the dry dust of exile. Slowly, with a resolve that seemed to crystallize in the very air around him, he nodded. His voice emerged steadily yet with an unmistakable edge of determination:

> "I will go. If the Ark is the key to confronting Nero, then I shall see this quest to its end—even if the journey takes me into the very heart of darkness."

With that solemn pledge, the council set forth their plan. Shalem meticulously marked a route to Elephantine on the map, his quill's scratch echoing like distant percussion amid whispered cautions. Baraqiel detailed the necessary provisions—supplies that retained the faint aromas of leather and dried herbs, guides whose silent footsteps blended seamlessly with the trade winds along the Nile. Tzefaniah, ever precisely, recited coded phrases that shimmered with secrets, each word layered with the promise of salvation.

As the morning wore on, the atmospherics in the chamber shifted. The air, once thick with apprehension, now vibrated with a sense of determined purpose. Yet beneath every careful word and every measured plan, there lingered the knowledge of what was at stake was a haunting reminder that failure would not only empower the Beast but shatter the fragile bulwark of hope that they had all so painfully built.

When the council slowly began to disperse, their careful footsteps echoing in the silent corridors, Abiram came to stand beside John. His gaze, somber as the first shadows of dusk, locked with John's.

"You have brought us to a crossroads, John. The path ahead is fraught with peril, but it is a path we must tread. The Beast will not wait, and neither can we."

John's eyes, reflecting both the golden glow of the dwindling morning and the steely resolve of his vision, softened in acknowledgment. "The visions have shown me that much, Abiram. The Beast may batter us with its cruelty, but neither shall the light be extinguished."

In that resonant moment, as the murmurs of the council faded and the stone chamber exhaled its centuries-old secrets, the Essenes of Qumran readied themselves for the weighty journey ahead. Outside, the desert wind carried the scent of a coming storm, mixing with the raw taste of anticipation on every tongue. The ancient walls, steeped in the memory of battles fought in both spirit and flesh, silently bore witness to their solemn vow: that, against all odds, the light would prevail over the encroaching darkness.

Chapter Seven
From Ponza to Rome

The Tyrrhenian Sea spread vast and glistening beneath the soft glow of dawn, its surface reflecting the faint blush of the sky. Ponza, with its jagged cliffs and rugged coastline, loomed ahead like a fragment of another world. The island was a stark, brooding silhouette rising from the water, its craggy cliffs veiled in morning mist. The air was thick with the tang of salt and the faint earthy scent carried from the grove of olive trees clinging stubbornly to the rocky hills.

The inlet was hidden, almost imperceptible from the open sea, its waters a deep turquoise that shimmered under the slanting rays of the early sun. It was a place of quiet isolation, untouched by the prying eyes of Rome's spies and soldiers. Waves lapped gently at the shore, a deceptive serenity that masked the storm of decisions and preparations that awaited the small gathering assembling there.

Abiram and John stood at the edge of the inlet; the two men cloaked against the chill sea breeze. John's gaze was fixed on the horizon where the sleek outline of a boat grew steadily larger. The silence between them was heavy, their thoughts weighed down by the enormity of the task ahead. This was no simple meeting, it was a turning point, a convergence of secrecy and risk that would determine the fate of their mission.

As the boat drew closer, the rhythmic creak of oars slicing through the water became audible, a sound that broke the uneasy stillness. The vessel itself was unremarkable, a weathered craft of modest size, yet it carried something far more valuable than its worn timbers suggested. Figures cloaked in Roman garb sat aboard, their postures rigid, their faces shadowed by hoods. They looked less like travelers and more like specters gliding across the water, silent and purposeful.

When the boat reached the shore, the operatives disembarked swiftly and with practiced efficiency. The leader, Lucius, stepped forward first. His presence was commanding yet wary, his sharp eyes scanning the surroundings with the vigilance of a man accustomed to danger. Behind him, two others worked to unload heavy crates from the vessel, their movements deliberate but strained. A third figure, a woman with piercing green eyes and an air of quiet menace, lingered near the prow, her hand resting on the hilt of a dagger.

Lucius inclined his head slightly, addressing Abiram with a tone that was brisk but respectful. "I am Lucius," he said. "We've brought what you asked for."

Abiram's gaze swept over the group, his expression betraying nothing. "And the Ark?" he asked, his voice low and steady.

Lucius hesitated, a flicker of unease crossing his face. "It is here," he said, glancing toward the crates. "But its journey was... eventful. There were complications."

Claudia, the green-eyed operative, stepped forward, her tone sharp and uncompromising. "Complications? More like bloodshed. Nero's agents are closing in. They know something is happening—maybe not everything, but enough to sniff around Elephantine like hounds on a scent." Her hand tightened on the dagger's hilt, her frustration evident. "We lost a man in Egypt. We barely made it out with the Ark intact."

Abiram's expression darkened, and he exchanged a look with John. "The Beast's shadow stretches farther than we imagined," he said quietly. "But the Ark is here. That is what matters now."

At Lucius's signal, the two operatives began prying open the crates. Each movement was deliberate, almost reverent, as though the act of revealing what lay within carried its own danger. When the final layer of cloth was peeled back, the Ark emerged, its golden surface glowing faintly even in the muted light of the inlet. Intricate patterns danced across its surface, shimmering as though alive. The cherubim atop the lid seemed to gaze into eternity, their outstretched wings forming a space that hummed faintly with a presence that could not be explained.

John stepped closer, his breath catching as he beheld the sacred vessel. The whispers from his visions returned, swirling like eddies in his mind, their meanings elusive yet pressing. "It is as I saw it," he said, his voice hushed. "A vessel of light, of power. The key to the battle ahead."

Claudia broke the spell with a snort. "A vessel of light won't mean much if it gets us all killed. We need a plan, and we need it now."

The group moved beneath the grove of olive trees, the sun climbing higher and gilding the gnarled branches with an otherworldly glow. The grove provided a fragile sense of privacy, though the tension among the gathered operatives rendered it anything but serene. A map of Rome was unfurled across a makeshift table, its edges weighed down by stones. The operatives clustered around it, their faces hard with determination and fear.

Lucius pointed to the Tiber on the map, tracing its meandering course with his finger. "Our operatives in Rome have arranged for a safehouse in the Subura district," he explained, his voice clipped. "It's hidden beneath an apothecary. Secure, but not invulnerable. The Ark will be moved there under cover of darkness."

Abiram nodded, his expression grave. "And from the Subura?"

Lucius's jaw tightened. "That's where things get more dangerous. The closer we get to the Forum, the closer we are to Nero's watchful eyes."

Claudia leaned forward, her green eyes flashing. "We'll need more than shadows to protect us. Nero's Praetorian Guard are everywhere, and they don't ask questions before drawing their swords."

John studied the map, his finger hovering over the Forum. "The visions showed me this place," he said quietly. "The heart of Rome, crumbling and in ruins. The Ark must be brought here, to this place of power. Only then can its light confront the Beast."

Lucius frowned, clearly unconvinced. "And how exactly do we confront the Beast, John of Patmos? Do we walk into the Forum and pray that the heavens split open?"

Abiram's voice cut through the tension like a blade. "The Ark is not a weapon in the sense you imagine, Lucius. It is a tool, a conduit for the divine. But it must be wielded correctly. With the Ark in the Forum, we can shift the balance—not through brute force, but through the will of heaven."

The conversation turned to logistics, the map becoming a battlefield of strategies and contingencies. Lucius outlined the routes into Rome, marking Roman checkpoints and safe passages. Claudia argued fiercely for multiple escape routes, her tone laced with urgency. Abiram insisted on the necessity of contacting their operatives in the Senate, speaking of the few senators brave enough to act against Nero.

As the sun climbed toward its zenith, the group's voices intertwined in a symphony of planning, debate, and resolve. Yet beneath the surface of their words lingered an unspoken fear—a shared understanding of the forces they were up against. The Ark lay at the center of it all, a vessel of immense power and even greater mystery. Its golden surface seemed to gleam with anticipation, as if it, too, awaited the fulfillment of its purpose.

As the meeting concluded, Abiram placed a hand on John's shoulder, his gaze steady but shadowed. "The path ahead is fraught with peril," he said. "But the light must prevail."

John nodded, his eyes lingering on the Ark. The whispers in his mind grew louder, their urgency undeniable. The Beast would not wait—but neither could they.

The faint light of dawn crept over the ancient port of Fiumicino, casting long shadows across the wharfs. Ships bobbed gently on the rippling waters of the Tiber as merchants shouted orders to unload cargoes of oil, wine, grain—and bananas. Among them, a modest-looking vessel moored quietly, its presence unremarkable amidst the activity. Yet within its hold lay not ordinary fruit but something far more sacred: the

Ark of the Covenant, its divine radiance concealed beneath layers of thick cloth and nestled into crates filled to the brim with ripening bananas.

Abiram and John stood near the edge of the dock, cloaked in the unassuming tunics and sandals of Roman merchants. They blended seamlessly into the chaos around them, their garb chosen to deflect suspicion as they worked to mask their purpose. The operatives Lucius and Claudia were close by, similarly disguised, their eyes darting toward every legionnaire that passed within sight. The faint scent of bananas mingled with the briny tang of the sea air, and the sound of distant hammers striking wood echoed faintly across the port.

"Keep your heads down," Abiram muttered under his breath as Lucius and Claudia approached the vessel. "Let the fruit speak for itself."

Claudia smirked, though her grip on her dagger remained firm. "Let's hope it speaks quietly, then."

The loading process was swift but fraught with tension. The crates were hoisted onto a cart, their heavy contents rattling faintly against the wood as the wheels began to turn. Two operatives disguised as porters guided the cart toward the cobblestone streets leading away from the docks, their movements brisk but deliberately unremarkable. John and Abiram followed at a distance, their gazes locked on the crates as though willing them to remain untouched.

The streets of Fiumicino bustled with activity. Vendors hawked wares from wooden stalls, their voices mingling with the chatter of passersby. Legionnaires patrolled the area, their polished armor glinting in the sunlight. Every glance from a soldier sent a jolt of apprehension through the group, though they maintained their composure, their disguises blending them into the crowd.

"Bananas for the emperor," Lucius murmured to a legionnaire as they passed through a checkpoint, his tone casual but pointed. The soldier raised an eyebrow but waved them on, uninterested in the mundane cargo. Claudia exhaled softly; her knuckles white as she gripped the edge of the cart.

As the group neared Nero's sprawling palace, the atmosphere shifted. The air grew thicker, laden with the scent of roasted meats and pungent spices wafting from the palace kitchens. The grand structure loomed ahead, its marble columns gleaming like fire in the midday sun. Within its walls, the chaos of the outside world fell silent, replaced by an eerie stillness, a silence weighted with power and danger.

The operatives moved toward a secluded entrance near the palace kitchens, their cart creaking faintly on the cobblestones. The kitchens themselves were a cacophony of movement and noise—cooks shouting orders, flames crackling beneath pots, knives flashing as they chopped. Yet beyond the main kitchen lay a quieter chamber, hidden from the bustle, where the bananas would be stored—and where the Ark would remain, if all went according to plan.

Claudia knocked twice on the heavy wooden door leading into the secluded chamber, her movements quick and precise. A servant opened it hesitantly, his eyes flicking toward the cart with curiosity. "Bananas for the feast," she said sharply, her Roman accent flawless.

The servant nodded, stepping aside to let them pass. The group entered the chamber, the door closing behind them with a heavy thud that echoed faintly against the stone walls. The room was dimly lit, its cool air carrying a faint metallic tang. Crates and barrels lined the walls, their contents varied and mundane. But as the operatives unloaded the crates of bananas, the tension in the room grew palpable, as if the air itself bristled with the weight of their secret.

Abiram approached the crate containing the Ark, his movements slow and deliberate. He rested a hand on its edge, his expression grim. "We are within the Beast's lair," he said quietly, his voice barely audible above the distant clatter of the kitchens. "The Ark cannot remain here for long."

John stepped forward, his eyes flicking toward the door. "We have no choice but to wait for nightfall. The visions showed me darkness and movement beneath the stars. That is when we must act."

Lucius shook his head, his brow furrowed. "Do you realize what you're asking? If Nero's men catch so much as a glimpse of this—if they suspect even the faintest whisper of treachery—we will all burn."

"And yet," Claudia said, her voice cutting through his protest, "we've come this far. The Ark is here. We can't falter now."

The tension in the room thickened as the operatives exchanged glances, their expressions a mixture of determination and fear. Every sound from the kitchens seemed louder, sharper, as if amplified by their unease. The faint rumble of footsteps outside the chamber sent a ripple of apprehension through the group.

John's hands trembled as he rested them on the crate, his lips moving in silent prayer. The whispers from his visions were louder now, insistent and haunting. He could see flashes of what lay ahead—the halls of the palace bathed in shadow, figures moving through the darkness, the glint of armor and the blaze of fire. The Ark was at the center of it all, a beacon of light that would either save them or consume them.

Hours passed, each one heavier than the last. The room grew colder as the sun dipped lower, its rays failing to penetrate the stone walls. The operatives stood vigilant, their eyes fixed on the door, their hands hovering near weapons hidden beneath their cloaks. The Ark rested silently within its crate, its divine presence palpable even in its concealment.

As dusk approached, Abiram stepped toward John, his expression etched with resolve. "When the darkness falls, we move," he said firmly. "This is the moment we've been preparing for. The Sons of Light cannot falter."

John nodded, his heart pounding. The whispers in his mind grew deafening, their urgency unrelenting. Nero's palace was a place of power, but it was also a place of vulnerability where the Beast could be confronted.

And as the light faded, the group steeled themselves for the night ahead, the air thick with anticipation and fear. The Ark remained at the center of it all, its golden surface hidden yet radiant, waiting for its moment to shape the fate of the world.

Chapter Eight
The Light of Judgment

The night carried an eerie stillness, a heaviness that clung to every stone and breath. Torchlight flickered along the vast corridors of Nero's sprawling palace, its flame-crackled whispers punctuating the oppressive silence. A disguised group of operatives pressed forward with purpose, their footsteps muted against the smooth marble floors. They moved as shadows, each step measured, as if the sound of even the smallest footfall might awaken the dark forces slumbering within these decadent halls.

At the heart of their covert operation lay the golden crate—a crate deceptively inconspicuous and, in its peculiarity, laden with significance beyond measure. Concealed within its ornate surface, behind a disguise of exotic bananas that rippled softly with each step, was the Ark. As it rumbled softly across the polished floors, every tremor in its journey was like a heartbeat—a sacred pulse echoing the destiny it bore. The air, already dense with the perfume of incense and burning wax, grew even heavier as they neared Nero's elusive quarters. An unnatural energy seemed to hover and prick at their skin, a palpable charge that set their nerves aflame. This was the seat of ultimate power and decadence—a domain where Nero twisted the world to suit his carnal whims, and where the darkness John had once envisioned had come to rest.

Before them loomed, the bronze doors leading to Nero's inner sanctum. Their surface glowed faintly in the dance of flickering firelights, engraved with scenes of conquest, indulgence, and vanity. The images depicted triumphant legions, oppressive victories, and sumptuous feasts—mocking the sanctity of faith and the purity of moral conviction. Lucius, his fingers flexing nervously as if they held a promise of both salvation and doom, stepped ahead. With careful, deliberate gestures, he signaled for the others to remain composed in silence. Claudia's eyes hardened like polished obsidian, her knuckles turning white as she gripped the hidden hilt of her dagger—a small but lethal reminder of the dangers that lay ahead. Abiram, ever the stoic guardian of ancient wisdom, adjusted the folds of his cloak; the weathered fabric whispered of bygone eras as he moved with gravitas and heavy anticipation. John lingered at the back, the chorus of whispered voices in his mind rising in a crescendo. Each uneven breath felt monumental, as though the very ground beneath them pulsed with the weight of the sacred vessel they struggled to carry.

They stepped into the chamber where Nero reigned. The grand hall was a study in extravagance: massive columns of pristine marble soared upward, supporting a vaulted ceiling where constellations of painted gold met the pungent scent of burning oils. At the far end, beneath a massive hearth whose flames cast long, twisting shadows, Nero reclined lazily on an opulent divan. His golden tunic shimmered like the façade of a deity, brilliant against the darkened hues of the room. With a casually raised hand and a goblet of dark, velvety wine in his grasp, his eyes met the group with a mixture of amused disdain and calculated curiosity. He embodied a ruthless arrogance—a tyrant who ruled from a throne forged of the blood and suffering of Rome, his very presence a testament to power and hubris.

"More offerings for the emperor," Nero drawled, his voice dripping with self-indulgence and mockery. "Tell me, merchants, what treasure have you brought this time? Another shipment from Egypt? Or perhaps some exotic fruits for my feasts?" His words seemed to dance in the heavy air, taunting and light.

A charged silence fell as the operatives exchanged furtive glances. Their hearts pounded in unison, each beat resonating like a war drum within the vastness of the hall. Then, with a composure honed through peril and devotion, Abiram stepped forward and bowed subtly. "A gift, my lord," he intoned, his voice steady yet laden with undercurrents of truth that shimmered with hidden fire. "Something worthy of your reign. Something unparalleled."

Intrigued, Nero tilted his head in measured curiosity. With the deliberate slowness of one accustomed to commanding awe, he rose from his sumptuous seat. His gaze narrowed, and he demanded, "Unparalleled? Very well. Show me." His tone was both a command and a challenge a gauntlet thrown at the feet of fate.

Lucius and Claudia, their hands trembling imperceptibly but with deadly precision, moved to unfasten the crate's lid. The room's hush deepened; every sound became magnified—the creak of aged wood, the rustling of fine cloth, and the soft exhalation of flames kissing the hearth. When the final protective layer was pulled back, the Ark was revealed in full, transcendent radiance.

The Ark shone like a beacon—a golden vessel that captured every flicker of firelight and refracted it into an ethereal brilliance that bathed the room in otherworldly glow. Its intricate patterns shimmered and rippled, as though alive, moving with secret purpose. Atop its lid, cherubim were carved with such exquisite detail that their outstretched wings and solemn expressions evoked both awe and awe-stricken fear. For an agonizing moment, nothing stirred except the silent, reverent heartbeat of the palace. Even Nero's swagger faltered; his smirk melted away, replaced by an expression of disbelief and an almost silent dread.

"What is this?" Nero murmured, his voice dropping in volume, now edged with an unfamiliar tremor. "A treasure? A relic? Tell me its power."

Locking eyes with the emperor, Abiram's response was firm and profound. "It is neither treasure nor relic, Nero. It is the divine—a beacon of light that transcends the power you claim to wield." His words, both a declaration and a warning, resonated like a tolling bell through the vaulted chamber.

Nero's arrogance surged in a desperate attempt to mask the flicker of doubt in his eyes. "No light can outshine the emperor of Rome!" he sneered, and at that moment his hand reached greedily toward the Ark.

The instant his fingers brushed its hallowed lid, a cataclysm ignited. The room exploded into a blinding flash of pure radiance a light so fierce, it seemed to rend the very fabric of existence. Shadows were obliterated in an instant, every hidden corner exposed in the searing clarity. The operatives were thrown backward by the blast, instinctively shielding their eyes from the overwhelming brilliance. In that same heartbeat, Nero's form convulsed; his golden tunic dissolved into the light as his body writhed grotesquely, collapsing inward until he vanished entirely, leaving nothing but a trembling, shimmering haze.

For a suspended moment, the silence that followed was more deafening than any clamor. The Ark pulsed once—a deliberate, measured throb—its radiance softening but never dimming. Its presence was undeniable, a force of nature, a divine wrath that had consumed Rome's most powerful man in but an instant.

And then, as quickly as the divine light had surmounted darkness, fire began to rage. It erupted first from the massive hearth, a burst of feral flames that leapt hungrily to the nearby tapestries and once-gilded statues. The opulent designs on the walls writhed under the savage blaze, their grandeur disintegrating into spirals of ash, molten fragments spilling like tears of a broken empire. The very marble beneath them trembled, groaning as fissures spider-webbed through its ancient surface. Fire spread like a living, ravenous entity, obliterating pride and opulence in its unstoppable march.

"Rome will burn," Abiram whispered solemnly as he turned to the group, his voice barely audible amid the escalating inferno. "The shadow of the Beast is no more—but the city will not escape its cleansing."

John sank to his knees, his hands clutching his head as the once-distant whispers in his mind surged into a cacophony of urgent voices. "It has begun," he murmured, his trembling voice a mix of terror and awe. "This is what I saw—a fire descended from the heavens, consuming all and birthing a new world in its wake."

Amid the chaos, the operatives scrambled to their feet. The palace corridors, once majestic and seemingly indestructible, are now convulsed under the onslaught of the inferno. Flame devoured columns and statues, reducing them to smoldering ruins. Outside the palace, the city of Rome erupted into pandemonium—flames leaped from building to building as the night sky was transformed into an ominous canvas of orange and red. The streets became tumultuous rivers of sound, filled with the terrified cries of citizens fleeing amidst the roar of destruction.

John's eyes, stinging with tears yet ablaze with determined conviction, turned once more to the Ark. Now less brilliant, yet still pulsating with a resilient glow, it remained a steadfast symbol of divine justice. "The Beast is broken," he breathed softly, as if uttering a sacred incantation. "And now, Rome itself must answer for its sins."

Before he could dwell further on these words, Lucius grabbed his arm, urgency sparking in his eyes. "There's no time to linger!" he shouted over the commotion, pulling John toward the exit as debris rained down from the collapsing ceiling. "Move now!"

The group fled through chaotic corridors, their movements swift and desperate. Servants and bewildered guards collided with them in the mayhem, their faces ashen with terror as the flames consumed the decadent palace. At last, they burst out into the open, where the banks of the Tiber provided a fleeting sanctuary. The river, its ancient waters glistening under the inferno's light, offered a momentary reprieve from the hellish scene behind them.

They gathered at the water's edge, staring in disbelieving silence as the once-mighty city of Rome was hunched under the weight of relentless fire. The skyline, once punctuated with triumphal arches and gleaming marble domes, had been reduced to a fractured silhouette of ruin. The glow of the inferno was both mesmerizing and horrifying—an almost grotesque beauty in its ruthless transformation, as though Rome itself was being purged by a cleansing, otherworldly force.

With the distant roar of the conflagration echoing across the Tiber, Abiram rested his hand resolutely on John's shoulder. His voice, though laden with sorrow, carried a steady beacon of hope. "This is the price of darkness," he declared. "But from these ashes, the Sons of Light will rise again."

John, his gaze fixed on the burning horizon, nodded with profound, bitter acceptance. "The visions have shown me this—the end of an era, and yet the birth of a new beginning. The Beast is no more—but our struggle is just beginning." His voice trembled with both grief and an unyielding resolve.

As the group melted away into the shadows of the ruined city, the divine Ark remained cradled in their care a spark of hope amidst devastation. The echoes of the fire, the ruined remnants of a fallen empire, and the shattered silence of what was once untouchable would linger as scars upon their memories. Yet in that darkness, they carried the promise of a new dawn light destined to shape the fate of the world.

Behind them, Rome burned—a fierce, transformative conflagration that would be remembered for generations as the night when darkness met its reckoning, and the eternal battle between light and shadow gained a force all its own.

Chapter Nine
The Last Bell

Late May wove a golden tapestry across the UCLA campus, bathing ivy-clad walls and sun-dappled courtyards in an amber glow. The air carried a hypnotic blend of sun-warmed parchment, distant ocean spray, and the subtle spice of coffee drifting from well-worn student cafés. But beneath the golden veneer of early summer, an unseen undercurrent stirred.

Inside Haines Hall, home to the anthropology department, the scent of aged wood and dust-dappled books mingled with the fading murmurs of a semester's end. The lecture hall held an almost ritualistic weight, as if thousands of lectures past had left behind faint echoes—whispers trapped in the beams and dusty corners.

Tonight, that weight felt different.

At its center, Professor Steve Kopper stood before his students, his worn leather journal resting at the edge of the desk, a relic of past expeditions. Its frayed edges carried the stories of lost cities, shattered temples, and secrets unearthed beneath foreign sands. Secrets that never quite let go.

His lecture had begun as an exploration of the Essenes—their ascetic doctrines, their war rule, their long-forgotten secrets. But there was something beneath the words, an unsettling thread woven into the lecture's cadence. Kopper felt it. The students felt it too, though they didn't know why.

"Consider the Essenes," Kopper intoned, his voice smooth yet weighted, as though each syllable carried centuries of untold stories. "Warriors and scholars both—custodians of a war rule forged in purity, discipline, and something far more elusive. My travels to Qumran have unraveled fragments of their doctrine, but even now, questions remain unanswered. Some are not meant to be answered."

A quiet hush followed.

"Professor Kopper, what's next? Will you return to Qumran this summer?" Alex Weller finally asked, leaning forward, sensing something unspoken.

Kopper hesitated.

A wry smile flickered at his lips, but his fingers absently traced the cover of his journal—an unconscious movement, the kind that spoke of a thought forming before the mind could catch it. "Ah, Alex," he mused, his tone teetering on the edge of revelation. "Qumran's paths have long been a second home, and there's still a chance I may return—pending the final funding approvals. The grants are in flux, and if they align, I could very well find myself back amidst the scrolls and desert winds. But if the finances don't fall into place, I may be drawn elsewhere."

He paused. His brow furrowed slightly—almost imperceptibly, but enough.

"Landsat satellite data has uncovered peculiar geological anomalies at Mount Shasta," he continued. "The formations whisper of treasure, perhaps a trove of gold concealed beneath its ancient bones. But it's not just the gold. The readings are... curious. The structural anomalies don't match geological expectations."

That last part landed heavier than intended. Kopper knew it.

The final bell tolled, a deep, resonant peal that did not merely signal the end of class but something larger, something shifting beneath the surface.

As students filed out, murmuring in tones that drifted between curiosity and dismissal, Kopper remained motionless, his gaze locked on the dust swirling beneath the glow of the fading sunset. He felt it again—the whisper of inevitability, the weight of a choice that wasn't his to make anymore.

Then, the door eased open.

His teaching assistant, precise and unobtrusive, stepped forward with a sealed envelope—the kind that bore no return address but carried the weight of unseen forces.

It wasn't thick, but it was heavy.

Kopper took it, fingers brushing over the edge like a scholar deciphering an artifact. The texture was wrong—it was cool, unnaturally so. A sudden flicker of something familiar—not memory, but something deeper, something unexplainable—rippled through him.

He hesitated—just for a breath—before breaking the seal.

As his eyes scanned the contents, his pulse slowed, as if something in him already knew what he was about to read. A shadow of intrigue flickered across his face, as if deciphering not just words, but a shift in fate itself.

The ink was faded, but deliberate.

The coordinates. The date. The signature.

A long silence.

Then—without hesitation, without doubt, without needing to read any further, he tossed the letter into the air, the parchment fluttering like a fallen prophecy.

"Well, I guess it's Shasta."

Already, his hand found his phone, fingers moving with unsettling precision. The choice had been made, but in truth, had it ever been a choice?

With deliberate certainty, he dialed the McCloud Inn, securing his three-week retreat. His words carried more than reservation—they carried a quiet submission to whatever had just been set in motion.

As UCLA settled into the hush of evening, Kopper exhaled, slow and measured.

The path had been chosen. The course had shifted long before he ever received that letter.

And in the looming shadow of Mount Shasta, something ancient whispered—pulling him forward, though the answers would not lie there.

They had never been there.

Chapter Ten
The Red Mustang

The engine of Steve Kopper's new 2026 Riptide Blue Eray Corvette purred along the winding curves of Route 5, slicing through dusk's amber and violet tapestry like a blade through silk. The sleek name "Eray"—a nod to the electric Stingray—captured its restless, electrified energy. Beyond the windshield, Mount Shasta loomed, a sentinel shrouded in legend and waiting to be deciphered.

Then, a flash of crimson cut across the landscape—a red Mustang streaking past, tearing through the beginnings of twilight, its roar slicing through the hush of the fading sun.

Kopper barely registered the movement before it was gone, swallowed into the horizon ahead.

The speed. The precision. The way it appeared, then vanished, too smoothly to be coincidence.

He allowed himself a wry smile, murmuring, "What's the hurry?"

The words hung in the air, unanswered.

Twenty minutes later, as he pulled into the parking lot of the McCloud Inn, a meticulously restored retreat nestled against Mount Shasta's sprawling foothills—the mystery took shape.

The Mustang was already there, its polished hood gleaming under the soft haze of the parking lot lights. He hadn't given it much thought after it vanished ahead on the highway, but now—here it was.

And the only open space left was right beside it.

Kopper rolled in smoothly, the Corvette settled into place next to the Mustang as if fate had dictated it.

Two beasts of the road. Two symbols of untamed speed.

He stepped out, stretching stiffened limbs, then leaned against his car, studying the scene with quiet amusement. "Well, what do we have here?"

The Mustang sat silent now, the taillights dark, the engine off.

Had the driver already gone inside? Or had they been sitting there, watching his arrival, waiting for the right moment?

Inside, check-in was routine.

The clerk offered the usual pleasantries, slid the key across the counter with easy efficiency, and pointed Kopper toward the stairs.

"Enjoy your stay."

Kopper nodded, pocketing the key, barely registering the words.

Simple. Ordinary. Unremarkable.

And yet—there was always something about the first night of a journey, wasn't there? The quiet moment before things truly began. The last stretch of normalcy before the road twisted into something unpredictable.

Maybe it was just the exhaustion talking.

He dismissed the thought and made his way upstairs.

Fatigue won out, pulling him under

He sat up, exhaling slowly.

The same question still lingered in his mind.

Who was in that car?

The two-hour nap had done its job. Steve Kopper woke refreshed, stretching out the residual stiffness from his drive before tossing on a clean shirt and heading downstairs.

The dining hall had transformed slightly since his arrival—soft candlelight flickering against polished wood, the hum of conversation blending with the clatter of silverware. The scent of grilled steak and buttered lobster teased the air, and Kopper barely glanced at the menu before ordering surf and turf.

As he waited for his meal, his gaze drifted across the room and landed on a sign near the small stage.

Tonight: The Klimkowski Sisters

The name struck a distant note of familiarity, but he couldn't quite place it.

A few minutes later, his plate arrived, a perfectly seared filet alongside succulent lobster tail. He sliced into the steak just as the room shifted lights dimming slightly, a hush falling over the crowd.

Then, the sisters stepped onto the stage.

Elaine Klimkowski and Diane Klimkowski carried themselves with effortless confidence. Their matching blue eyes and golden blonde hair caught the stage lighting just right, illuminating their presence with something more than just showmanship.

Kopper hadn't expected to be captivated, but there was a quality in their movements, in the way they worked the crowd, that made it impossible to look away.

Elaine, in particular.

The sisters had a storied history—television appearances dating back to their teenage years, a Hollywood resume laced with everything from acting to professional wrestling. They had been dancers on Star Search in 1987, models on NBC's Let's Make a Deal in 1990, and actresses in Problem Child 2 in 1991. Even their time assisting with illusions—working alongside The Masked Magician in Breaking the Magician's Code—was etched into entertainment history. And then, in

1999, they made their debut in professional wrestling as Lolli and Pop on World Championship Wrestling.

Now, they commanded the room with nothing but microphones and charm.

As they moved through the crowd, weaving between tables with playful banter and effortless vocals, Elaine looked at Kopper.

A fraction longer than expected.

A flicker of something unspoken.

And Kopper felt it immediately. Electricity, undeniable and unprompted.

Elaine held the moment just long enough to make sure he noticed, before moving on, her voice threading back into the performance.

When the set ended, she didn't hesitate.

Elaine strode directly toward him, her confidence cutting through the room like a blade through silk. She stopped at his table, gave him a knowing smile, and asked, "So when are you going to ask me to sit down?"

Kopper leaned back slightly, raising his brow in amusement.

"When you allow me to buy you dessert."

Elaine grinned, sliding into the seat across from him.

Small talk came effortlessly, their words were easy and light, charged with that unspoken energy lingering between them.

Kopper didn't press for details, didn't ask why she had singled him out.

Then, Diane appeared, her expression half-amused, half-practical.

"We've gotta put the equipment away," she reminded Elaine, giving Kopper a glance like she knew something neither of them did yet.

Elaine exhaled, casting one last look at him before standing.

Kopper watched her go, then tossed a casual remark after her.

"I'm staying a few weeks. Maybe we can meet up later."

Elaine glanced back, a smile teasing the edges of her lips.

"Maybe."

Little did Kopper know how soon that meeting would come.

And that danger would be involved.

Chapter Eleven
Dawn on the Shasta Trails

Morning broke with a sumptuous display of light and aroma at McCloud Inn. The first blush of dawn bathed the rustic retreat in warm hues, filtering through lace curtains with a soft golden glow. Outside, mist curled lazily over the foothills, dissipating as the rising sun stretched its fingers across the landscape. The air carried crisp purity, scented faintly with the damp earth of the mountain and the distant whisper of pine needles rustling in the breeze.

Kopper woke to the gentle chime of a vintage clock, its rhythmic ticking a soothing companion to the world's slow emergence from slumber. Unlike the road-weary exhaustion of the previous day, he felt refreshed, his muscles loose, his senses sharp. The bed, a masterpiece of old-world craftsmanship with its thick quilted comforter, had lulled him into deep, undisturbed sleep, something increasingly rare in his life of constant movement.

He rose, stretching away the remnants of sleep, and made his way downstairs to indulge in a breakfast that rivaled the decadence of the setting. The intimate breakfast room, a jewel of polished wood and delicate porcelain, hummed with quiet morning activity. Sunlight glinted off brass fixtures, casting amber pools over crisp linen tablecloths.

Spread before him was a feast: fluffy scrambled eggs rich with cream, crisp bacon shimmering with golden juices, freshly baked artisan bread still warm from the oven, accompanied by locally churned butter, its pale-yellow softness melting at the slightest touch. A steaming mug of freshly brewed coffee rested beside the plate, its dark liquid releasing waves of earthy richness tinged with notes of roasted hazelnut and bittersweet chocolate.

As Kopper savored each bite, the inn's owner—a fixture of quiet authority and warmth—approached with a knowing smile.

"Morning, Steve," he said, patting Kopper on the shoulder with the ease of old acquaintances. His weathered face, lined by time and tempered by the mountain air, carried the twinkle of someone who had seen many travelers come and go, each carrying their own stories, each leaving behind another thread in the inn's long tapestry.

They exchanged lighthearted quips, their conversation easy, familiar—rooted in years of Kopper's seasonal returns.

"You hear about the gold rumor again?" the owner mused, pouring himself a fresh cup of coffee. "Some fool up the ridge swears he found a vein last week."

Kopper chuckled, shaking his head. "There's always a new fool. Maybe this time, it's me."

The man's laughter was deep and knowing, rolling through the room like distant thunder.

Finishing breakfast, Kopper donned his Indiana Jones ensemble—rugged khakis, a sturdy leather belt with well-worn pouches, thick-soled hiking boots laced with precision, and the weathered fedora that had seen more dust storms, underground passages, and near misses than most artifacts ever would.

The mountain called to him, its steep inclines and wild terrain promising revelations only found in the footprints of those willing to chase them.

His ascent was measured, each step pressing into the earth with intent. The well-worn trail, framed by wild pines and scattered quartz, led toward the heart of the legend—a place where the whispers of hidden caves and abandoned claims still lingered in the wind.

The lore of Mount Shasta had long since embedded itself into the town's identity. Stories of unexplained disappearances, ghostly lights flickering high above the peaks, and old prospectors muttering about gold hidden in ancient volcanic veins gave the mountain an allure that stretched beyond geology.

One tale, in particular, had always fascinated Kopper—a rumor of an underground city buried beneath rock and time, its golden veins untouched since the days of the great California gold rush.

As he rounded a bend in the twisted trail, the road below revealed a familiar sight.

The red Mustang was there.

Its sleek form rested at the roadside, positioned in a way that felt neither incidental nor inevitable—just strangely timed. Kopper exhaled, amusement flickering at the edge of his lips.

"Well, what do we have here?" he murmured.

His investigation had led him to this exact target area, where fact and folklore collided in a game of wits against the mountain's secrets.

Parking his Corvette next to the Mustang—a ritual that now carried the faint scent of cosmic synchronicity—he began his descent toward the valley below.

It was then, nestled in a sunlit clearing painted with wildflowers swaying in the mountain breeze, that he spotted her.

Elaine.

She moved with a quiet grace, gathering delicate blooms with an absentminded ease, lost in the rhythm of the moment. Her golden hair, kissed by the morning light, framed the sharp angles of her face, accentuating the deep blue of her eyes—eyes that had lingered on him just a little too long the night before.

Before he could call out, his gaze flicked past her.

A shape moved in the trees.

A hulking silhouette slipping between the shadows, its steps unnaturally silent for something of its size.

A bear.

Its presence was neither hurried nor hesitant—it stalked forward with a careful calculation, as though weighing its interest in the lone woman standing amidst the wildflowers.

Kopper's instincts kicked in.

He murmured low, deliberate sounds, shifting his posture slightly—no sudden movements, just a signal, a subtle warning.

Elaine lifted her head, and their eyes met in an instant of perfect understanding.

Then, she turned.

Her body stiffened, her grip tightening around the fragile bouquet, but her movements were measured—controlled. She backed away, one slow step at a time, mirroring the bear's tension.

It held its gaze a moment longer, then—without incident—pivoted, disappearing into the thick forest beyond.

The breath neither of them realized they were holding finally exhaled.

They reconvened near the cars, a lingering silence settled between them before Elaine finally broke it.

She cocked her head, studying the Corvette with evident appreciation. "I wondered who owned that machine—it looks fast just sitting there."

Kopper smirked. "At first, I thought you were the comic book hero—the Flash—that zoomed by me yesterday."

She laughed, a bright sound that chased away the remnants of tension. "Had to get back to Diane for rehearsal," she said, but her gaze flicked back to the mountain with something deeper.

A knowing look.

"But what were you doing out here?"

Kopper sidestepped her question.

Instead, he reached into his satchel, pulling out a set of stereo pairs—tools of his trade. With quiet enthusiasm, he launched into an impromptu geology lesson, explaining the peculiar rock formations, the seismic whispers hidden beneath the surface, and the centuries-old quest for gold that had left this land riddled with secrets.

Elaine listened, intrigued—not just by the history, but by Kopper himself.

After the morning's near-miss, the promise of a hearty meal seemed more enticing than ever.

"Let's head back to the inn for lunch," Elaine suggested. "Today's special is shepherd's pie."

Back at the inn, as they settled into the warmth of conversation and shared meals, Kopper leaned in with a playful grin.

"Your room or mine?"

Elaine laughed. "Mine has a sister taking a nap. What do you think?"

Their words carried an undertone—something unspoken, something waiting.

Four hours later, as the afternoon light softened, Kopper made a quiet proposal.

"You only work two nights a week, right?"

Elaine smiled, considering. "And holidays."

"How about you join me in prospecting for gold, and we split everything equally?"

A pause. Then, she grinned.

"Sounds like trouble."

Little did they know—trouble was already waiting.

Chapter Twelve
The Dry River of Gold

Morning arrived with an unhurried grace, spilling golden light over the quiet sanctuary of McCloud Inn. Sunbeams filtered through lace curtains, tracing delicate patterns across the aged wooden floors, and the scent of freshly brewed coffee mingled with the crisp mountain air drifting through the half-open windows.

At a corner table, Steve Kopper sat, his weathered khaki shirt and battered field hat a testament to the countless expeditions behind him. Spread before him were the tools of his trade a trusted metal detector, a collection of well-worn notebooks brimming with sketches and data, and a finely tuned handheld XRF analyzer. Each item carried the silent weight of past discoveries, whispering of ancient roads traveled and mysteries unearthed.

Across from him, Diane sat, dressed casually in jeans and a soft sweater, her blue eyes gleaming with quiet amusement. Though she would not take part in today's excursion, her presence added an easy familiarity to the morning—one built on years of twin intuition with Elaine. She stirred her coffee absently, watching as her sister appeared at the top of the stairs with confident stride.

Elaine had dressed the part.

A rugged work jacket, durable boots, even a hat that bore a striking resemblance to Kopper's own—if one were to chase legends and flirt with fortune, one might as well embrace the aesthetic. She descended the stairs with a smirk, sweeping an exaggerated glance at his attire before remarking, "Well, if we're going treasure hunting, I figured I should at least look the part."

Diane chuckled, leaning back in her chair. "By the way, Indiana Joan, where's your bullwhip?"

Laughter echoed briefly between them, a fleeting moment of levity before the true adventure began.

A short while later, the Corvette's engine growled to life, carving through the winding roads of Mount Shasta as Elaine studied the vibrant Landsat satellite images glowing on the mounted screen. Shifting patterns of rust-colored iron oxide stains and the faint signatures of hydrothermal activity painted a digital map before her eyes—a silent cartography of buried secrets.

"These coordinates aren't just random patches," Kopper explained, his finger tracing clusters of spectral data. "The mineral composition here, especially the iron oxide streaks and quartz vein patterns, tells a story—a gold-bearing zone shaped by an ancient glacial stream."

Elaine's gaze remained fixed on the display, captivated. "So, the 'Dry River of Gold' isn't just some legend. It's real etched right into the terrain."

Kopper nodded, a flicker of quiet excitement beneath his composed expression. "I've always believed that every gold deposit hides a history—not just one of geology, but of people who sought it, civilizations that depended on it. When my research on Qumran lost funding, I found solace in pursuits like this—where science and mystery weave together."

As they neared their destination, the landscape shifted—towering pines gave way to jagged rock formations, and the road narrowed into a rough-hewn path that led to a canyon mostly forgotten by time. The entrance, masked by thick ivy and the natural camouflage of dense foliage, was barely noticeable to those unfamiliar with the terrain.

Stepping into the crisp air, Kopper felt the weight of history pressing against his senses—the murmur of an ancient glacial stream reduced to a faint trickle along the canyon floor. Every rock, every vein of quartz seemed to carry whispers of an era long past, waiting for careful hands to decipher them.

Walking carefully, the pair advanced along the uneven path, their metal detectors humming with quiet precision. Elaine ran her fingers over the layered stone formations, reading their textures like a storyteller unraveling an old myth. "Every fault line, every fissure—it all seems deliberate," she mused. "Like nature left us a coded message."

Kopper exhaled, nodding. "These deposits—the iron oxide, the parallel quartz—they aren't coincidence. They follow the path of the ancient stream, leaving behind clues that might guide us straight to what we're searching for."

Then, the silence shattered.

A sharp beep from the detector sliced through the canyon's hushed majesty.

Elaine knelt swiftly, brushing away a century's worth of moss and sediment. And there it was—gold, gleaming against the stone, catching the fleeting sunlight in an electric burst of brilliance.

Kopper retrieved the XRF analyzer, holding his breath as he scanned the sample. The numbers confirmed what instinct had already told them.

"Ninety-nine percent purity," he murmured, almost in disbelief. "This isn't just gold—we're looking at a major deposit, following the course of that ancient stream."

For a long moment, neither spoke, absorbing the weight of their discovery. Elaine's voice was softer now, thoughtful. "It's as if the earth has been waiting for someone to listen. Each nugget—it's more than just gold. It's a message, a map left behind."

Kopper's gaze darkened with intrigue. "History, much like geology, is layered. Sometimes, it takes years for the right hands to uncover the truth."

The canyon, bathed now in the glow of midday light, seemed almost alive—every rock, every shadow playing its role in a grand design far older than either of them.

They documented each finding, recording coordinates, tracing mineral concentrations, and searching for any sign of ancient inscriptions. Every beep of the detectors, every glittering fragment of quartz carried the promise of another clue, another step toward an untold story.

But as they packed up their gear, Kopper pulled out a scale, carefully weighing their haul.

Almost five ounces of gold.

Elaine blinked, stunned. "That's nearly ten thousand dollars—just from today."

Kopper nodded, closing the scale with a deliberate snap. "And this bed goes on for more than a mile. We have to put a lid on this. Loose lips sink ships."

Elaine hesitated, biting her lip. "It'll be hard to keep this from Diane. We share everything."

Kopper glanced around the canyon, his voice carrying the faint edge of caution.

"Then minimize it. At least for now. You never know who might show up."

Unbeknownst to them, those words would soon prove prophetic.

Chapter Thirteen
On the Gold Road

The echoes of the ancient, dry stream still clung to their senses as Steve and Elaine climbed into the Corvette, the scent of damp earth and quartz dust lingering on their clothes. Outside, the landscape bathed in the pastel hues of twilight, while inside, the soft glow of the digital dashboard illuminated their quiet triumph—five ounces of gold, the promise of something much larger beneath the surface.

Steve's steady hands gripped the wheel as the engine purred, a low hum underscoring their whispered plans. Nearly ten thousand dollars' worth of shimmering bounty sat carefully packed away—a discovery forged through ingenuity, persistence, and the relentless pursuit of something greater.

Elaine exhaled, her thoughts tangled between exhilaration and the quiet fragility of their secret. "Our legacy deserves a modern-day vault," she mused, fingers tapping absently against her knee. "There's a Chase Bank on Morgan Way in Shasta with impeccable safety deposit boxes."

Steve nodded, his voice low and thoughtful. "We'll secure our find well before anyone notices what we're doing," he murmured, his words swallowed by the hum of the car as they moved along the winding mountain roads, golden light dissolving into shadow.

The McCloud Inn awaited them at dusk, its timeless presence offering a sanctuary of nostalgia. Over a modest dinner, Elaine leaned back, a fond smile curling at the edges of her lips. "Our connection here goes deeper than just a place to stay. My father and his best friend grew up in Asbury Park, New Jersey—joked about playing volleyball with Springsteen on the beach back in the '70s."

Steve chuckled, shaking his head. "Bossland indeed."

The warmth of shared memory settled between them, a quiet reinforcement of trust in the glow of dim lighting.

Later, in the common room, the Klimkowski sisters took to the stage. Their voices wove a story—playful, nostalgic, and rebellious—each note echoing the deeper rhythms of adventure they carried in their bones. As Elaine moved effortlessly through the performance, she cast Steve a fleeting glance, something unspoken passing between them, something tied to the weight of discovery and the thrill of the unknown.

Morning arrived bright, the scent of coffee and warm pastries filling their room. Over scrambled eggs, crisp bacon, and golden toast slathered in butter, they murmured about the work ahead. Two weeks. A relentless expedition through rugged outcrops and secretive canyons.

And the land rewarded them.

The metal detectors whispered promises of fortune. Each dawn found them tracing patterns in ancient sediment, following the spectral cues hidden within quartz veins and iron oxide deposits. Every measured beep of their devices carried an intensity that stretched beyond mere exploration—it was the pursuit of history itself.

By the fourteenth day, they stood in stunned silence at what lay before them.

Steve flipped through his logbook, eyes darting over hurried calculations. "Elaine, this isn't just luck—we've cleared almost two thousand ounces." He glanced up, his expression both awed and serious. "That's about four million dollars sitting in our hands."

Elaine blinked, adjusting the weight of their newfound reality. "This feels impossible—like spearing apples in a barrel."

Steve grinned, eyes glittering with triumph. "No, Elaine—only hard science got us here."

Their laughter drifted into the wind, marking the culmination of their grueling yet exhilarating odyssey.

With their extended quest complete, the Corvette roared to life once more, carrying them toward Shasta—toward Chase

Bank, where their treasure would be locked behind steel and secrecy.

On the way to Weed, ten miles south of Mt Shasta, Elaine leaned back, eyes tracing the unfolding horizon. Soon, a modest sign emerged against the clear sky:

"Approaching Weed."

She smirked. "I wonder if they have an Easy Wider store there as well."

Steve laughed, shaking his head. "We'll find out."

The town was a quaint contrast to the wilderness they had conquered—weathered storefronts, familiar faces, and the scent of fresh coffee mingling with mountain air. As Steve parked near a cluttered workshop, the door swung open, revealing a lean man with sharp, inquisitive eyes.

"Steve, always a pleasure." His gaze flicked to Elaine. "And you must be Elaine—I'm Arbogast, but most folks call me Arbo."

Elaine offered a polite nod.

Steve moved swiftly, retrieving a duffel bag from the Corvette and setting it atop a sturdy wooden table. As the zipper unfurled, golden nuggets tumbled onto the surface, catching the workshop's dim light in dazzling flashes.

Arbogast's brows lifted in amusement. "Secret spoils, huh?" He reached for his industrial scale, letting the numbers settle with deliberate precision.

A beat of silence.

Then a low whistle.

"That's nearly four million in gold." His eyes twinkled. "Cash, or shall Granny be satisfied with a few crumpets?"

Steve's hearty laughter filled the space. "Just a check, Arbo. We'll deposit it at Chase."

That evening, over a quiet dinner at Arbogast's home where timeworn tools mingled with aged wine and warm conversation, their discussion moved effortlessly between reminiscing about past geological expeditions and contemplating the future.

Elaine leaned back, her fingers brushing the rim of her glass. "Feels like this is just the beginning."

Steve met her gaze, something unreadable flickering in his expression. "It is."

Even as the day's final light faded, neither could shake the feeling that their journey was far from over. That somewhere—beneath rock and time—another secret awaited.

And soon, someone would come looking.

Chapter Fourteen
Purposeful Evil

The Corvette surged into the night like a harbinger of destiny, its engine purring a promise against the dark void of the unknown. Steve and Elaine, buoyed by a triumph that defied expectation, rode the wave of success with an intensity that bordered on the prophetic. Each victory—both tangible and elusive—whispered of buried treasures and unimaginable power. Yet as they embraced possibility, unseen shadows slithered in the periphery, foretelling a fate steeped in calamity.

In the modest glow of an inn where music and laughter intertwined like a finely tuned symphony, Steve's thoughts danced with anticipation. He recalled the magnetic allure of Elaine and her enigmatic twin sister Diane, whose impending performance radiated confidence and mystery. That delicate harmony was put on pause when an unanticipated figure stepped into the light.

Father Pedro Armillas—an elderly man whose lined features bore the weight of secrets—glided toward Steve's table with an urgency that prickled the air. His fingers trembled slightly as he leaned in, his breath carrying the faint scent of aged parchment and something more—fear.

Without wasting time on formalities, Armillas spoke with a tremor of dread. "Doctor Kopper, I must confide in you," he murmured. "I am being tracked by a man—Father Roberto Samarelli—a relentless force from within the clandestine Sons of Mithras. They hide truths that transcend time itself." Each word dripped with warning, igniting a pulse of fear that Steve barely contained behind a calm exterior.

With the precision of a master cryptologist, Armillas recounted a tapestry of clues: an ancient carving of Robert the Bruce at Rosslyn Chapel, the murky intrigues swirling around Armillas in Rome, and the groundbreaking work of Victor Vargas amidst the sun-bleached ruins of Santorini. "Your Qumran dig was shut down because these forces—these evil powers—deemed the risk too great. They know how bright you are and how close you might be to discovering their greatest secret," he confided, his voice laden with regret and peril.

"Meet me tomorrow, away from prying eyes, and we will unravel this conspiracy."

With no performances scheduled for tomorrow night, Steve suggested a discreet meeting, and Armillas agreed.

Before a plan could fully coalesce, an ominous presence materialized from the haze.

Samarelli emerged like a specter drawn from a forgotten legend—an imposing figure whose features, chiseled and severe, exuded a cold malice. In an instant, the camaraderie at the table turned to stark alertness.

Armillas's eyes widened in recognition. "It is him!" he hissed, his voice barely a whisper but heavy with dread as he ducked down. "Signal me when he vanishes into the shadows."

A charged moment passed as Steve subtly acknowledged the signal and confirmed his readiness.

"Until tomorrow," came Armillas' curt farewell—a promise that would soon unravel as an unforeseen darkness crept across the lands beneath an ominous sky that now enveloped Mt. Shasta.

At daybreak, Steve and Diane resumed their quest in the hidden canyon, their shovels biting into earth to yield another bountiful vein of gold. The thrill of discovery was tempered by the lingering specter of Armillas' dire warning. Yet nothing could prepare them for the pandemonium that greeted their return to the McCloud Inn.

The lobby teemed with police, their radios spitting disjointed dispatches that snapped the fragile veneer of normalcy. In the midst of cracking tension, a single, shattering decree froze their blood.

Pedro Armillas had been murdered.

His cryptic revelations were not idle secrets—they had marked him just as he had predicted, and now those connected to him stood in line for the same unspeakable retribution.

Seeking refuge, Steve and Elaine fled to their room, only to find their sanctuary had been desecrated.

The space lay in ruins, as if a wild, unseen force had torn through it, leaving chaos in its wake. Among the wreckage, a torn photograph fluttered atop the scorched sheets—an image of Diane and Elaine from years ago, its edges singed as if touched by fire.

Every shattered item and scorched surface spoke of a threat that was both immediate and relentless. Steve's acute eyes combed the destruction, while Elaine's normally steady gaze wavered with a dawning terror.

The scattered clues—Rosslyn Chapel, Cardinal Rausch, and Santorini—formed a mosaic of danger, intricately intertwined with history's darkest secrets.

As the shock subsided, practicalities asserted themselves with grim inevitability.

"This journey is no longer optional," Steve declared, his tone resolute despite the undercurrent of fear. "It will cost us dearly—but today's haul alone is more than enough to cover it."

Elaine's steely nod was accompanied by a wry remark. "We've already banked four million in gold. Our tracks are covered. Also, who would believe that tale about a golden goose farm in Redding you gave Arbo?"

Together, they secured passage from San Francisco to Edinburgh, their resolve hardening with every word.

The descent into Edinburgh was marked by a dense, almost palpable tension. Renting a sleek Jaguar, they embarked on a drive through Scotland's rugged highlands, where nature's raw beauty was interlaced with the promise of hidden answers and lurking threats.

As the car wound its way toward Rosslyn Chapel, the ancient edifice loomed ever larger—a relic of sacred mysteries and forbidden lore, its timeworn stones murmuring long-forgotten secrets.

In the early morning, they finally stood before the chapel.

Its silhouette, carved against the fading light, evoked a sense of awe and foreboding in equal measure. The towering spires cast jagged shadows in the waning light, the air thick with damp stone and the remnants of whispered prayers.

Here, within those venerable walls, lay the potential to dismantle the enigma—or to plunge them further into peril.

With hearts pounding in sync and minds racing through possibilities, Steve and Elaine braced themselves for a confrontation that promised to demand a far greater toll than they had ever imagined.

Their path was singular, the choice irrevocable.

The muses deemed it so.

Chapter Fifteen
Whispers from Rosslyn Chapel

The last remnants of dawn clung to the horizon, casting long, flickering shadows across the Scottish Highlands as the Jaguar XKE cut through the mist like a blade. The sleek machine hummed with restrained power, carrying Steve and Elaine deeper into the heart of a mystery that had lurked beneath centuries of dust and deception.

Their departure from the McCloud Inn had been swift, their passage through San Francisco measured by quiet calculations and whispered urgency. Now, with their gold secured and their path laid bare; they had traded the wild frontier of Mount Shasta for the ancient echoes of a land that held secrets far older than even the most coveted veins of gold.

Elaine adjusted in her seat, her fingers tracing lazy circles on the leather dashboard, the steady drum of rain against the windshield adding a rhythmic pulse to their unspoken thoughts. A knowing glance passed between them—unspoken yet fully understood. Their journey had shifted from fortune to fate.

Steve's grip tightened around the wheel as the narrow road curved along a steep ridge, and through the thinning mist, Rosslyn Chapel loomed ahead.

It did not emerge. It revealed itself.

Gothic spires clawed toward the sky, their silhouettes twisting against the amber glow of sunrise. Worn carvings kissed by centuries, clung to the walls like a forgotten language waiting to be read. The air grew thicker, charged with something unseen, something ancient.

Elaine exhaled sharply. "There it is."

Her voice was quiet, reverent—tinged with both apprehension and awe.

Steve didn't respond. He simply slowed the car, pulling onto the gravel path, where the crunch beneath the tires felt deafening against the stillness of the moment.

They had arrived.

Inside the sanctuary, shafts of penetrating light revealed a labyrinth of timeworn surfaces. Every chisel mark and spiral-carved motif pulsed with clandestine energy, as if the chapel itself were a living archive, guarding secrets that yearned to be revealed. Steve mused that this was not merely a building but an alchemical convergence of myth and history.

Elaine, too, felt a deep, almost electric connection to the silent whispers echoing from every shadowed corner.

A docent, attired in muted tones that echoed the chapel's solemn grandeur, greeted the few remaining visitors with a calm, authoritative presence. "Welcome to Rosslyn Chapel," she intoned, her voice resonating softly off the ancient walls, each syllable measured like a chant in an age-old ritual. "Since its construction in the 15th century, this sanctified space has served as a crucible of myth and history. Legends of the Knights Templar, secret codes interwoven in these carvings, and whispers of treasures hidden in plain sight have captivated seekers for generations."

As she guided the group along the echoing nave, the measured cadence of her footsteps on timeworn flagstones punctuated her narrative, setting hearts racing and igniting dormant passions for mystery.

Near a secluded alcove, partially shrouded by time and shadow, stood an exquisitely detailed effigy: the head of Robert the Bruce.

"Observe this relic," she murmured, her words dripping with reverence as shivers cascaded through the gathered crowd. "The great King of Scots is immortalized here not only as a symbol of power but as a guardian of hidden truths. Many believe that his likeness conceals clues to an ancient legacy—whispers of secrets which may well include treasures once destined for the mysterious shores of Oak Island.

At that charged moment, Steve's pulse quickened with an intensity that melded adrenaline and awe, while Elaine exchanged a conspiratorial glance with him—a silent vow that their shared destiny was binding them to this very mystery.

As the tour neared its conclusion, the docent announced a one-hour luncheon break—a customary pause in the continuous flow of historical revelation that left the chapel corridors momentarily unguarded. One by one, the other guests departed, their echoing footsteps receding into the vast silence.

The weight of centuries and the promise of forbidden knowledge coalesced around Steve and Elaine. They were alone.

Seizing the decisive window, they slipped quietly into a secluded corridor away from any prying eyes. In that profound quiet, every sensory detail was amplified: the chill of the stone underfoot, the soft murmur of distant echoes, and the unyielding rhythm of their racing hearts.

Steve braced himself, pressing against the cold stone with steady force. His muscles tightened as he coaxed the carved effigy into motion, his breaths shallow and measured. The soft scrape of rock against rock sent a tremor through the silence—then, with agonizing precision, the head shifted. A whisper of dust spiraled into the air as the compartment revealed itself, undisturbed by time.

Inside lay a small, timeworn scroll—a silent testament to secrets guarded through the ages. Its wax seal, etched with a sigil unmistakably linked to clandestine orders both revered and feared, confirmed every whispered rumor and half-spoken legend that had led them to this moment.

Elaine's heart pounded in synchrony with Steve's as they exchanged one final, loaded glance—a mutual, unspoken vow that this remarkable discovery was the indispensable cornerstone of a much larger quest.

No sooner had they secured the precious clue than the distant shuffle of the docent's approaching footsteps shattered the silence—a stark, sudden reminder that even ancient secrets demand a toll for their revelation.

Elaine's pulse thundered in her ears as the sound of approaching footsteps grew sharper, closer. Her eyes locked onto Steve's, silent communication passing between them in an instant—this had to be perfect. The scroll was secure, the effigy restored, but there was no erasing the tension in the air.

They had uncovered something meant to remain hidden.

Now, getting out was the real test.

Chapter Sixteen
Two Close for Comfort

Elaine's eyes widened as she stood just a few steps away from Steve near the open, arched entrance of Rosslyn Chapel. Outside, a dark Land Rover glided to a halt in the dew-softened morning light, its headlights briefly illuminating a glint on the wet pavement that vanished as mysteriously as a half-remembered dream. Peering through the open doorway, she immediately recognized the chilling silhouette of Father Samarelli—the very man whose cold involvement in Father Pedro Armillas' death at the McCloud Inn in Shasta had long haunted her memories. In that moment, fragments of her past floated unbidden: a flash of a stage performance shared with her sister Diane, where the man's eyes, cold and calculating, had promised retribution. Her pulse throbbed with a mix of dread and unyielding determination.

Without a moment's hesitation, Elaine's voice rang out, sharp and clear: "Stage left—Samarelli!" Her finger, steady despite the turmoil inside, snapped toward the ominous figure. Steve's gaze met hers, and in that shared look lay years of silent understanding and internal conflict. He recalled that haunting memory—each detail fueling his resolve. In a silent, calculated retreat, they slipped through the left-side door toward their sleek Jaguar, its engine purring with the promise of swift, quiet escape. As they vanished into the dense Scottish morning, an uneasy uncertainty clung to the air—a secret message left for them in that fleeting glimpse that begged more questions than answers.

Safely at speed on the winding approach of a secluded country road, Elaine's anxious whisper broke through the engine's steady resolve: "There's no way he could have known we were here." Her voice held a note of incredulity that mingled with memories of past encounters, when a mere hint of danger had changed everything in a heartbeat. Steve's eyes remained fixed on the serpentine path ahead, his tone measured yet edged with intrigue. "Or perhaps he knew about the clue as well," he replied thoughtfully, the word "clue" carrying an extra weight that hinted at hidden layers yet to be uncovered. Elaine, her voice suddenly trembling with both fear and a fierce determination born from countless close calls, declared, "The heat is on now."

In that fleeting moment of uncertainty, Steve paused and mused aloud, "Let's ignore that mystery for now. We need to decide our next move quickly—do we head back to the airport, or is there another way out? We're left with just two options: left or right." Almost providentially, as if the fates conspired in cryptic whispers, a weathered sign materialized in the distance. Its faded, bold letters proclaimed "Loch Ness," and as though echoing some long-forgotten legend, a chill passed over them. For a split second, disbelief and amusement danced in their eyes. "Some choice—Nessie or Samarelli?" Elaine teased, letting a brief note of humor puncture the tension. With a wry smile, Steve replied, "Ironically, this is the very definition of a Hitchcockian McGuffin—never predictable at all."

Merging onto the M9 and later the A82, the Jaguar sliced through the undulating highland roads on a grueling 140-mile journey that Tarzan might envy. Along the way, as the Scottish landscape unfurled in a montage of glistening lochs and fog-bound peaks, Steve hesitated for a moment to open the cryptic note found in the head at Rosslyn Chapel. "Would you do me the honor?" he asked. "Sure," replied Elaine with a knowing smile that carried both hope and trepidation. When the note was unfurled, Steve joked, "So, what does the fortune cookie say?" Elaine read softly, "Be at Apocalypse Cave during an Aegean Storm to hear a message." Underneath the levity, however, a subtle disquiet lingered as if that message was a promise of further peril. Miraculously, despite their notorious lead-footed reputations, the duo completed the 140-mile trip in a swift 133 minutes.

Their destination unfolded near Fort Augustus, where The Inch Hotel—an imposing country lodge with roots as a rustic hunting retreat and later as an RAF base during World War II—stood regally against the legendary loch's misty backdrop. Elaine's meticulous research had arranged a diversion tour right on her cell phone, ensuring that this detour would offer both respite and a renewed perspective on their tumultuous quest. Inside, plush lounges exhaled warmth, and the comforting crackle of log fires provided solace from the chill of the Highlands. After a quick check-in, they refreshed themselves with a warm shower and even managed a brief, restorative nap. Soon, they gathered for a quintessentially Scottish meal sprawled on rustic oak tables. The savory aroma of haggis with tender neeps and tatties mingled with the rich, smoky flavor of Cullen Skink, while delicately pan-fried Scottish salmon and a decadent serving of cranachan—whipped cream, honey, raspberries, and toasted oats crowned with a subtle hint of whisky—told tales of culinary lore from centuries past.

Over the hearty fare, amid the gentle clinks of cutlery and whispered toasts to future exploits, Steve steered the conversation to their next move. "We should book a flight to Rome from Edinburgh," he proposed thoughtfully, his eyes reflecting both determination and the cumulative weight of their dangerous mission. "All we know about Cardinal Gustav Rausch is just his name—he might be our golden cup or simply another red herring." Elaine's gaze darkened with both resolve and a trace of vulnerability as she agreed, adding, "And beyond that, there's a direct flight to Santorini. Canaves Oia Suites & Spa looks enticing. Shall I lock it all in?" With a confident nod, Steve affirmed, "Absolutely." Their plans spun out like threads of fate, pulling them inexorably toward the next stage of their enigmatic quest while hints of deeper conspiracies shimmered just beneath the surface.

After a blissfully late sleep and a robust Scottish breakfast featuring fluffy scrambled eggs, thick-cut bacon, the famed square Lorne sausage, hearty haggis, delectably crisp tattie scones, and perfectly buttered toast, they set out on a tranquil boat tour destined for the storied Urquhart Castle. A mellifluous narrator recounted the enigmatic lore of Loch Ness—detailing ancient Pictish carvings, a fabled 7th-century encounter with Saint Columba and a mysterious water beast, and even a 1933 flurry of sightings spurred by the notorious "surgeon's photograph," now long debunked. As the boat ride drew to a close, their tour meandered to a quirky Nessie gift shop, where Steve, with a wry, self-aware smile, remarked that perhaps the true monster was not lurking beneath the waters but hidden within the artful marketing of a legend. Elaine's uncontrollable laughter broke the tension for a moment, a fleeting spark against the ever-present darkness of their journey.

   Their detour complete, they returned to the airport for a peaceful flight—an interlude from the escalating perils that had marked every step so far. Upon arriving in Rome, the pace shifted dramatically. Renting a scarlet Ferrari, they navigated through Rome's bustling, ancient streets and parked near Cardinal Rausch's office on Via della Conciliazione. The vast, open square before them hummed with the echoes of antiquity, the cobblestones whispering secrets of long-departed eras as they began their cautious trek. Suddenly, as if fate itself had summoned him, a creaking door swung open and out stepped none other than Samarelli. In an instant, the moment shattered—Elaine's heart lurched as she grabbed Steve's arm and spun him around. "It's him—the red herring option!" she exclaimed, her voice a mix of disbelief, terror, and defiant humor. Steve, suppressing a grim smile, murmured, "Yes, Elaine, but apparently his visual acuity does not match yours." The brief encounter in Rome, heavy with portent and unexpected twists, was a stark reminder that their enemies were as elusive as they were deadly, and the mystery was far from over.

   After four nerve-wracking hours navigating the labyrinthine square, the stage was set for the next leg of their odyssey. As dusk yielded to night, they boarded another flight—this time toward the sun-soaked shores of Santorini. With each passing moment, their hearts bore the weight of every secret unraveled and every unresolved clue. Amidst the glimmer of Mediterranean twilight, their adventure pressed onward—a tapestry woven of history, danger, mystery, and destiny too profound to ignore.

As the flight descended, a crackling radio broadcast in a language half-forgotten and tinged with static cut through the cabin—a final, mysterious note leaving them to wonder if forces beyond their comprehension were still at work. With that, the threads of their quest tightened, the promise of yet another revelation lingering in the charged silence.

What new enigmas might the ancient ruins of Rome or the mythic allure of Santorini reveal? In the quiet spaces between calculated moves and adrenaline-fueled chases, the mystery deepened, leaving every page imbued with the promise that the truth, however elusive, was ever within reach—and that their next move might just change everything.

Chapter Seventeen
The Shaking Earth

The low hum of the Ryan Airlines cabin pulsed like a muted heartbeat, barely masking the tension that permeated every fiber of the aircraft. Elaine's eyes remained locked on her phone as she navigated a maze of digital scans and archived bulletins—a labyrinth of data that hinted at secrets too vast to ignore. Among these faded records, one name shone with a cruel irony: Father Samarelli, once the beloved pastor of Blessed Trinity Catholic Church in Ocala, Florida. In his heyday, his gentle sermons and earnest words had been a beacon of hope; now, covert forum posts and deteriorating digital archives revealed a disturbing transformation—from a shepherd of souls to a man veering into shadow. Cryptic symbols, a fragmented image of a tarnished crucifix from his old church door, and unsettling annotations coalesced into an ominous portrait of betrayal and occult intent.

As the aircraft began its descent toward Santorini, the melodic resonance of Blessed Trinity's once-hopeful chants mingled with Elaine's foreboding thoughts. Every digital clue seemed to echo with the possibility that the very foundations of an institution she once revered were now steeped in deception—a betrayal that spanned continents, from sunny Florida to the ancient, cobbled streets of Rome.

Touching down on a sunlit runway that shimmered with mythic promise, Steve and Elaine were whisked away in a sleek, obsidian sedan. The winding road led them to The Canaves Oia Suites & Spa—a modern Cycladic haven perched dramatically on rugged cliffs. The hotel's pristine whitewashed walls and expansive glass panels framed a living canvas of the restless Aegean below, while the distant caldera loomed like a silent sentinel of forgotten lore. In their suite, a private infinity pool appeared to merge with the horizon, offering a transient moment of sumptuous calm amid a tempest of revelations.

That evening, inside the intimate confines of Petra Gourmet Restaurant, the space transformed into both refuge and confessional. Over a sumptuous lobster bathed in saffron-infused butter and accompanied by ethereal strains of stringed music, Steve leaned forward, his voice measured, yet charged with urgency.

"Elaine, the details we uncovered during our flight are merely the opening act. What else have you found about Samarelli's transformation after those early days at Blessed Trinity?"

Elaine's eyes flashed with unyielding resolve and a shadow of old pain as she replied, "In Rome, Samarelli was remade. He wasn't simply the gentle pastor once admired—he was seduced by a clandestine sect known as the Sons of Mithra. They repurposed the very virtues that once endeared him to his flock, twisting them into instruments of ruthless control. This wasn't just a career change; it was a metamorphosis into a life marked by secret rituals and merciless dogma." Her voice dropped even lower, as if sharing a forbidden secret. "And then there's his brother, Kapelli—a ghost lurking in the financial underbelly, orchestrating a labyrinth of shell companies and phantom transactions. Their network spans from the pews in Ocala to the secret chambers of Rome, all woven into an intricate web of global deceit."

Steve's gaze darkened as the implications settled over him like a shroud. "So, the corruption runs deeper than we imagined, where faith and vice intertwine in an empire of silence—and of extortion. It's a conspiracy that spans not just continents, but centuries." The flickering candlelight danced over his face, every shadow a reminder that the truth was as elusive as it was dangerous.

The next morning, soft light streamed through the floor-to-ceiling windows of The Canaves Oia Suites & Spa, gilding the breakfast nook with warm amber hues. Amid

"Dr. Kopper, I've been following a thread that some claim intertwines modernity with ancient sacred history," Vargas confided, his tone low and urgent. "Consider the legend of the Ark of the Covenant and its alleged exile to Elephantine Island. In Jerusalem's most turbulent periods, some records whisper that the Ark was secreted away from Solomon's Temple for safekeeping. Elephantine, with its vibrant yet enigmatic temple and its rare papyri, may well have been the hiding place of that forgotten relic." He paused, letting his words soak in. "I suspect your funding was cut not by chance but by forces desperate to stifle such revelations. They will stop at nothing to keep these truths veiled."

A heavy silence enveloped the group as distant excavators droned on and the ancient wind whispered through the ruins. Steve's face darkened with reluctant understanding, while Elaine's hand clenched in silent, determined defiance. "It seems," Steve murmured, "that those in power, those who fabricate myths for control, will do anything to ensure the truth remains buried." Lowering his voice to a conspiratorial whisper, he added, "The Sons of Mithra have already silenced dissent—Father Armillas being a grim reminder. If we persist, they may come for us next."

Later that day, with plans evolving rapidly, Elaine scrutinized her phone and spoke in a hushed, determined tone, "If cramped airflights aren't viable, there's the Oia Santorini pristine white linens and delicate porcelain, Steve and Elaine shared a quiet meal punctuated by the occasional buzz from Elaine's phone—a reminder that danger still lurked in the digital shadows. Leaning forward, she asked, "What is it about Santorini that calls to us so profoundly?"

Steve slowed, his eyes drifting over the rugged volcanic cliffs plunging into the restless Aegean. "Santorini isn't just a marvel for the eyes—it's a living chronicle of secrets. Akrotiri, for instance, preserves a sophisticated Bronze Age civilization that vanished in a volcanic cataclysm. Those intricate frescoes and finely wrought pottery speak of a lost world, as if the island itself serves as a bridge between myth and history." His voice softened, laden with the gravity of centuries. "It whispers of ancient hubris and the divine judgment that silenced them—of secrets waiting to be unearthed."

After breakfast, the pair wandered the ancient pathways of Akrotiri, the salty tang of the sea mingling with the musty aroma of buried ruins. Their destination was a meeting with Dr. Victor Vargas, the acclaimed archaeologist whose previous collaborations with Steve had hinted at deeper, global enigmas. Amid the soft clatter of excavation tools and the distant echo of scholarly debate, Vargas emerged from a cluster of researchers—tall, resolute, and with an expression that shifted rapidly from cordiality to grave concern.

Helipad, just five minutes away. It's steep at $3,900, but it promises a rapid route to the Skala Helipad in Patmos—under an hour, if we're lucky." Within ninety minutes of hurriedly packing, they were airborne toward Patmos—the legendary isle that cradled the legacy of John, the author of Revelation. Elaine's phone buzzed intermittently with cryptic messages and news clippings, each one hinting at a global conspiracy that wove through history like a dark thread.

Yet, the narrative of their journey was far from linear, appearing almost random. Within their charged silence, the threads of their quest grew ever tighter—a tapestry woven from betrayal, occult alliances, and global conspiracies that spanned centuries.

In the space between calculated moves and adrenaline-fueled chases, the mystery deepened. Each cryptic clue and every whispered confession promised that the truth was tantalizingly close—a truth liable to shatter sacred institutions and redefine the balance of power. With every heartbeat, Steve and Elaine edged closer to unlocking secrets hidden in plain sight, as ancient forces and modern intrigues converged.

Chapter Eighteen
The Choking Whisper

The sleek helicopter sliced through churning, salt-laden skies as it descended toward Skala, where Patmos unfurled like an ancient map, its intricate contours steeped in mystery and myth. The rotor blades drummed a relentless cadence that fused with the briny tang of the sea and the metallic hint of an impending storm. Elaine's heart raced in sync with the powerful thump of the engine as they neared the helipad. Her eyes sparked with a mixture of determination and wonder when she pulled up her phone to pinpoint their next refuge—Patmos Aktis Suites & Spa. Nestled upon a windswept cliff overlooking Grikos Bay, the hotel's alabaster façade shimmered against a bruised twilight, its pristine Cycladic architecture standing as an ode to refined elegance and enduring tradition.

As they disembarked, a world of sensory marvel greeted them. Inside Patmos Aktis, cool marble floors echoed with whispers of bygone eras, each measured step resonating like the beat of an ancient drum. The lobby unfurled like a living symphony—plush velvet furnishings embraced visitors in sumptuous warmth; freshly laundered linens caressed the skin with understated luxury; and the gentle murmur of a fountain punctuated the space with timeless cadence. Over the next three days, Steve and Elaine immersed themselves in the island's rich tapestry. Mornings began with the bitter, robust aroma of freshly brewed Greek coffee and delicate, flaky pastries that crumbled at their touch—a sensory reminder of traditions nurtured by time and sea. Afternoons found them strolling sun-drenched streets, where every tactile encounter—from the warm, weathered stone of ancient alleyways to the rough-hewn charm of hand-carved market stalls—spoke volumes of history, passion, and secret lore.

Their explorations gradually revealed layers of Patmos that stretched far beyond its inviting beauty. At the Monastery of Saint John, they wandered through corridors where frescoed walls pulsed with divine revelation, and Elaine's fingertips traced gentle contours of sacred art amid an atmosphere thick with the musty aroma of centuries-old incense. In one secluded chamber, a solitary mural depicting a tempest-tossed figure amid a cavern stirred deep emotions, hinting at both loss and rebirth. Later, in a lively taverna carved into a rocky alcove, a weathered fisherman's gravelly voice recounted the legend of the Cave of the Apocalypse, describing how the cave would tremble and come alive under violent storms, its ancient walls imbued with an unyielding, sacred energy.

By the third evening, the sky darkened to an obsidian void and the calm was shattered by an impending tempest. A palpable electricity danced in the wind, carrying with it a chill that penetrated even the most stalwart souls. The previously serene Patmos Aktis was transformed as mighty gusts shook expansive windows and relentless sheets of rain hammered the polished stones of the terrace. With a silent, shared resolve, Steve and Elaine abandoned the hotel's luminous sanctuary. Their footsteps splashed through slick, rain-soaked cobblestones as they advanced purposefully toward a destiny that lay beyond everyday safety.

The Cave of the Apocalypse loomed ahead like a jagged scar upon the hillside dark wound set against a lightning-streaked sky. As they stepped into that cavern, every sensory detail was magnified: the cool, clammy texture of ancient rock beneath their fingertips; the rhythmic drip of condensation echoing through the dark; and the crunch of each footfall reverberating like a heartbeat in the hollow chamber. Amid the ceaseless roar of the storm outside and the low, pulsing hum rising from the cave's hidden depths, a voice emerged from the darkness—neither entirely human nor fully spectral—that breathed a single, weighted phrase: "Tana Kirkos." The sound etched itself into the cold, moss-covered walls as though carved by time itself—a promise, a threat, or perhaps both. In that charged moment, with rain still streaming down their flushed faces, Steve and Elaine exchanged a knowing glance. The mysterious utterance was far more than mere words; it was a tangible, visceral beacon urging them toward a destiny that stretched beyond the turbulent Aegean. Far away, hidden amidst legend and shadow, lay the mythic Tana Kirkos Island in Ethiopia—a fabled sanctuary where long-dormant secrets awaited rekindling.

When the tempest subsided into a haunting, intermittent lull, the cave's damp breath clung to them like a shared secret. They lingered in the cavern's silent embrace, each lost amidst rising thoughts of ancient forces and ominous omens. Steve's mind raced with implications while Elaine's heart pounded, caught between fear and exhilarating resolve, as the mysterious aftermath promised revelations yet to come. Emerging from the cave, shivering from both the residual spray of salt and rain, they paused on the rain-slicked steps leading back to civilization. Even as they retreated into the comforting warmth of Patmos Aktis, the enigmatic words and the storm's charged energy refused to dissipate—echoing in their minds as a foreboding drumbeat.

That night, sheltered in the quiet elegance of their suite, Elaine revisited the cryptic message on her phone. The esoteric call to "Tana Kirkos" had grown into more than a mere clue; it was a link in a chain that spanned continents—a connection between the mystical histories of the Aegean, the religious intrigues of Rome, and the clandestine empires operating in distant lands. Meanwhile, Steve spread old documents and news clippings across a polished desk, remarking that that single phrase might be the thread that, if pulled, would unravel a vast tapestry of betrayal, occult alliances, and ancient power struggles. In whispered debates and heated discussions that stretched deep into the night, punctuated occasionally by a wry laugh—their camaraderie a buoy amid rising dread—they began to map out their next moves. Elaine half-joked, "Who knew a fabled island in Ethiopia would be the perfect antidote to a Greek tempest?" Even as their laughter rang out, the stakes were unmistakably high.

When dawn broke over Patmos, the storm had eased, leaving behind an air of hushed expectancy. Light seeped into the room, turning white linens and polished surfaces to gold, as they savored a modest breakfast of traditional Greek fare—each sip of strong coffee and every bite of flaky pastry steeped in quiet contemplation. The chaos of the previous night lingered like an unfinished symphony—a reminder that they were irrevocably bound to a cause stirring with forces beyond control. By mid-morning, a decision was reached. With renewed resolve and palpable urgency, they packed their essentials. Elaine's phone displayed the route to Patmos's

Skala Helipad—and the cost of a rapid transfer was noted, an investment into a future shrouded in mystery. As they hurried into the waiting vehicle, the soft hum of the engine mingled with the distant murmur of the sea, and the island's rugged beauty slowly receded, replaced by the promise of a larger voyage. A journey that would lead them from the storied coasts of Greece to the mythic secrets of Tana Kirkos in Ethiopia, as each passing moment synchronized their heartbeat to a purpose that was as mysterious as it was irresistible.

Chapter Nineteen
The Levis's Golden Seraphim Wings

The journey began where destiny and revelation collided—on the storm-battered shores of Patmos. After their harrowing encounter in the Cave of the Apocalypse, Steve and Elaine wasted no time. A sleek helicopter awaited them, its rotor blades slicing through the salt-laden air as it soared upward, carrying them away from the turbulent isle. Below, Patmos receded into the vast expanse of the Aegean, its rugged cliffs and crystalline waters diminishing into the distance like a tempestuous dream, while scattered emerald islands sparkled in the sunlight like fragments of forgotten antiquity. Their next destination was Athens—a city where modern civilization hummed in vibrant contrast to the echoes of an ancient world. The helicopter touched down with precise grace, and the duo quickly merged into the bustling energy of the metropolis; yet there was no time for contemplation of Athens' storied past, as a chartered jet awaited at a private terminal to launch them toward an entirely different slice of history.

"It's a race against time," Elaine noted, her tone resonant with both resolve and urgency. As the jet's engines roared to life, they ascended high above the earth, carving a direct route over the shimmering Mediterranean. Beneath them, cobalt waters yielded to tawny sands—patchworks of wind-sculpted dunes whispering of lost empires and ancient caravans. Enclosed within the jet's cabin, the atmosphere thrummed with tension as Steve meticulously traced their route on a weathered map. "We're retracing the trade arteries of the ancient world," he explained, his voice carrying the gravitas of centuries past. "Centuries ago, these skies bore caravans laden with knowledge, goods, and spiritual beliefs, journeys that have echoed into our present time."

The miles melted away in a mesmerizing interplay of azure horizons and golden sunsets. Hours later, the jet descended upon Addis Ababa, Ethiopia's vibrant capital and the gateway to mysteries that beckoned. From high above, the city unfurled as a vivid mosaic—a dynamic blend of domed churches and sleek modern high-rises, bustling streets alive with motion and punctuated by the rich aromas of roasted coffee, wood smoke, and exotic spices. Street vendors rose with voices echoing like ancient calls amid a symphony of honking tuk-tuks and rustling traditional attire, each swirling fabric a testament to Ethiopia's enduring cultural heritage.

Their guide, a wiry local with sharp, observant eyes and a knowing smile, ushered them to a rugged 4×4 parked just beyond the urban clamor. The vehicle rumbled along narrow, winding roads that gradually led them from the kinetic energy of Addis Ababa into the serene, undulating wilderness of Ethiopia's highlands. Here, as twilight bathed lush rolling hills in a cool, ethereal glow, acacia trees with spindly branches stood as silent sentinels against the encroaching night. The rugged trail carried them higher, and with each mile the air thinned and grew crisper—whispering promises of secrets held by the ages.

As darkness settled, the headlights of the 4×4—aptly christened "The Highland Sentinel"—revealed a vast panorama of Lake Tana, its waters glistening like obsidian under the watchful gaze of a luminous moon. The lake's deceptive stillness pulsed with silent, hidden histories. At its edge, a modern vessel known as "The Eternal Whispers" awaited. Its sleek silhouette offered a striking contrast to the age-worn natural beauty around it. Boarding the boat, they were soon greeted by Bruce Halbridge, director of the Quest Institute and an esteemed colleague from Steve's academic past. With calm authority and scholarly gravitas, Bruce explained in measured tones, "According to ancient Ethiopian tradition, the Queen of Sheba's legendary visit to King Solomon not only forged a royal union but also gave birth to Menelik I—the founder of Ethiopia's illustrious Solomonic dynasty. Legend even tells us that Menelik journeyed to Jerusalem and returned bearing the Ark of the Covenant, thereby linking Ethiopia irrevocably with the divine legacy of Solomon." His words painted Ethiopia as a chosen land, steeped in a sacred heritage that transcended time, as nearby traditional tankwas—papyrus boats whose designs had scarcely changed over centuries—glided past like spectral echoes of history.

Their ultimate destination loomed ahead: the enigmatic island of Tana Kirkos, rising from Lake Tana like a venerable guardian of secrets. Shrouded in mystery, its access was concealed by a thick curtain of overhanging foliage, as though nature itself sought to keep its ancient lore hidden. The Eternal Whispers anchored at a discreet distance, and Steve, Elaine, and Bruce transferred to one of the traditional tankwas. The gentle creak of papyrus and the rhythmic splash of paddles set a measured cadence, marking each deliberate stroke as they ventured into the heart of the unknown stillness where the scent of damp earth mingled with the ancient aroma of weathered stone, and the soft rustle of leaves whispered timeless legends. Abba Levi, the island's revered spiritual leader, awaited them—clad in simple, timeworn robes that spoke of humility steeped in unwavering conviction. With measured grace, he extended a callused hand in welcome, and his calm authority immediately instilled a deep sense of trust. Guiding them through the island's inner sanctum, Abba Levi unfolded the sacred heritage held within its core; in the temple treasury, relics emerged like murmurs from an age long past—a gleaming bronze gomer, evoking memories of ancient rituals and sacrificed souls, and a resplendent bronze breastplate adorned with twelve lustrous jewels, each symbolizing one of the tribes of Israel. As the venerable Abba Levi placed the breastplate upon himself, its radiant brilliance ignited the dim space with an ethereal glow, while a richly painted tapestry depicting Moses and the creation of the Ark unfurled before them, its vivid strokes breathing life into the hallowed tales of Exodus.

With deliberate cadence, Abba Levi spoke of the Ark as imparting a sacred truth. "The seraphim wings—for they are more than symbolism—generate a delicate balance of energies that neutralize destructive forces. Sparks of divine electricity emanate from them, serving not only as a guard against pretenders but as a beacon for the faithful." Steve's breath hitched as he leaned in, quietly inquiring, "Where, then, does the Ark reside?" With solemn gravity, Abba Levi responded, "It lies hidden beneath the Church of Our Lady Mary of Zion in Axum." Elaine and Steve exchanged a stunned glance, the enormity of this revelation resonating profoundly. Yet Abba

Levi continued, hinting at a whispered legend of a secret tunnel carved into the rugged ridges overlooking Axum—a clandestine passage connecting to the basement of the ancient church. Promptly, Elaine pulled out her iPad to trace the terrain on Google Earth, collaborating with Abba Levi until they pinpointed a shadowy, indistinct cluster that suggested a possible route; each input on her iPhone deepened the tantalizing mystery.

With their time on Tana Kirkos drawing to a close, twilight melted into indigo night as they departed for Bahir Dar to catch a flight to Axum on Ethiopia Airlines. Every moment of the journey, now imbued with fervent urgency and haunted by lingering secrets, nudged them ever closer to the fabled church and the ultimate mysteries of the Ark. The odyssey, seamlessly interlacing the storied coasts of Greece with the enigmatic heart of Ethiopia, pulsed with the promise of ancient truths waiting to collide with modern destiny.

Chapter Twenty
The Electric Wings Spark

The journey from Bahir Dar to Axum was an immersion into a living canvas—a realm where modernity and the echoes of antiquity brushed together in sublime chiaroscuro. Touching down at the austere Axum Emperor Yohannes IV Airport, its timeworn façade bearing the solemn codes AXU and HAAX, Steve and Elaine felt as though they had stepped into a masterfully aged fresco, each moment steeped in the mystique of forgotten empires. Outside, a rugged Nissan Patrol—its body dusted with the relics of ancient paths—waited like a steadfast steed, poised to traverse landscapes that whispered in the language of sun-scorched stone and elusive secrets.

Their arrival marked only the prelude to a meticulously rendered three-day odyssey. At the Atranos Fantasy Hotel & Spa—nestled among narrow lanes where every weathered wall seemed to murmur tales of time—the duo found only a transient refuge. Carl Koenig, the concierge with eyes like deep pools of ancient wisdom, greeted them with a measured smile, silently acknowledging the gravity of their quest even as he checked them in. That initial day, wrapped in the quiet rituals of survival, unfolded with the tender insistence of destiny. In a bustling market dedicated to the art of preparation, every mundane transaction transformed into a rite of passage as they hand-selected a robust tent with secure stakes, warm sleeping bags, cushioned pads, and a portable stove paired with neatly sealed fuel canisters. Non-perishable sustenance—canned goods, energy bars, and dried fruits—became tangible talismans against the encroaching unknown.

At the soft blush of dawn on the next morning, they embarked on an illuminating pilgrimage to the Church of Our Lady Mary of Zion. This venerable sanctuary, a monumental citadel of stone, rose like a grand composition from an age-old epic. Colossal walls, hewn from blocks as perfectly aligned as brushstrokes on a timeless canvas, reached skyward. The primary barrier radiated an almost sacred luminescence in early light, while a secondary rampart funneled the way into slender corridors guarded by exquisitely carved motifs of regal lions and watchful canines. These chiseled guardians—born of master artisans' genius—evoked a profound sense of divine protection, a visual hymn celebrating the intermingling of spirituality and force. As they wandered beneath the ancient arches, the lingering words of Abba Levi—spoken with solemn conviction at an earlier gathering—seemed to animate the very stones, hinting at hidden tunnels and secret passages concealing the Ark of the Covenant. Every echoing step promised to reveal profound, concealed truths.

Yet the tranquility of their pilgrimage was soon shattered. In the cool predawn hours, as Axum's labyrinthine alleys danced with shifting light and shadow, Elaine ventured out alone—only to be confronted by the ominous presence of Father Roberto Samarelli. His measured, predatory steps emerged amid the interplay of dusk and sunrise, a dark figure that disrupted the serene palette of Axum with a stark brushstroke of impending danger. Elaine's heart pounded like wild percussion, every beat resonating with ancient warnings. Instinctively, she retraced her steps through the silent, storied streets and hurried back to the safety of the hotel.

Inside the subdued glow of the Atranos lobby, Elaine's whispered confession—"Samarelli is here"—cracked the fragile calm like a discordant note in a long-forgotten melody. In that moment, urgency replaced caution. With a few resolute words, they contacted Carl Koenig and arranged an expedited checkout. In a swift flurry of hushed coordination, they pared their belongings down to the essential provisions; every item was chosen as a silent pledge to the trials ahead. Although most supplies were already packed in the SUV, they had to forgo their accumulated food stores—a sacrifice no one wished to make, but one that was necessary in the pursuit of forbidden knowledge.

The Nissan Patrol roared to life once more, its engine a constant, rhythmic heartbeat beneath the brooding twilight. Guided by meticulously pre-planned GPS coordinates, the vehicle carried them to the very cusp of a perilously charged terrain—a threshold that was said to conceal the fabled tunnel's opening. Under a sky bleeding deep indigos and burnt oranges, they temporarily halted their escape. Here, far from the protected confines of the hotel, they set about crafting their own ephemeral sanctuary. With nimble precision, they unfurled a compact tarp and erected a temporary shelter; amid a quiet flurry of activity, they gathered dry wood. Their deft movements breathed life into a modest fire—a dance of flickering flames whose warm glow defied the encroaching darkness. As dynamic shadows played over their determined faces, the small blaze became both a beacon of hope and the prelude to deeper mysteries waiting just beyond.

Haunted by ancient whispers and the heavy memory of Father Samarelli—the dark figure whose predatory calm had shattered their earlier serenity—Steve and Elaine knew it was time to leave Axum behind. The Nissan Patrol's engine thrummed with urgency as they navigated rugged, dusty paths into the wild, uncharted highlands rising like silent sentinels above the sacred city. After a tense drive through rocky outcrops and crumbling ruins, they reached a secluded clearing nestled among weathered olive groves. Here, under a vault of stars and the cool, anticipatory hush of night, they set up camp. Their tents were pitched with deliberate care, and a modest fire was kindled—a solitary flame amid the ominous dark. In that uneasy stillness, memories of Axum intermingled with the specter of Samarelli, and the charged night air granted them a brief, restless sleep until the promise of dawn would beckon them onward.

At first light, the camp stirred with a tentative routine. A hearty breakfast of sizzling bacon, eggs, coffee, and toasted bread offered a fleeting return to modern comforts, even as the shadows of ancient enigmas loomed large in their thoughts. With the warmth of the meal lingering on their tongues, the duo turned their attention to the rugged hills before the realm where nature itself guarded long-held secrets. Guided by both instinct and the unwavering pulse of a GPS set against the timeless quality of the land, they began the arduous task of cutting and clearing thick brushes to reveal what nature had hidden for so long.

Laboring under a rising sun, each swing of their tools and every necessary pause for water reinforced the urgency of their search. At last, their determined efforts unveiled a gaping hole in the earth hidden opening obscured by layers of rocks, debris, and soil accumulated over millennia. With shovels in hand, they excavated meticulously until a flat stone door emerged from the earth's embraced surface worn smoothly by the passage of time and inscribed with unspoken incantations from ages past.

Steeling themselves, they armed their high-powered flashlights and carefully descended a narrow, winding path carved deep into the darkness beneath the land. Every step was laden with uncertainty; every pause to shift stubborn debris was a silent admission that they were trespassing on hallowed ground where forgotten forces dwelled. Soon, however, an insurmountable barrier appeared—a colossal stone that abruptly blocked their path. "Well, what's next?" Elaine whispered, her voice trembling with equal parts fear and determination. Steve studied the massive monolith, murmuring, "There must be some kind of hair-trigger mechanism." In a stroke of fate, his hand brushed against an unseen button; a solitary, resonant click shattered the silence as the colossal stone rotated exactly ninety degrees, revealing a six-foot hand-hewn wooden door reinforced with glinting metal supports with the ominous the Ark of the Covenant bolted across the door.

The interior glowed with the flickering light of oil lamps. A narrow stairway ascended to an upper chamber. To the right was a weathered wooden table that lay crowded with delicate papyri. With apprehensive reverence, Steve unrolled each ancient scroll. One document—a codicil to the Book of Revelation—ominously warned that an ancient evil, long subdued by John and the Essenes, could one day break free. Another recounted how John of Patmos had once sought the Essenes' aid to stave off the apocalypse, while yet another detailed how the Ark, procured from Elephantine Island, had been employed to capture the malignant essence of Nero. When Steve's voice dropped to a hushed murmur— "So this is what Dr. Vargas was talking about"—the full weight of destiny pressed upon them.

For a brief, charged moment, fate demanded their undivided attention. Steve gingerly stepped toward the ornate door and pressed his eye to the keyhole. In that glimmering aperture he beheld an endless sea of shimmering, molten gold treasure that whispered of fortune and divine promise. Elaine moved closer and, when she too peered in, her heart hammered at the sight of a golden snake coiled languidly around an ancient, gnarled tree. Their eyes met in that electrifying instant, each reflecting the internal battle of avarice and foreboding. Finally, with a tremor in her voice heavy with both awe and reproach, Elaine murmured, "Steve, can't you see? It's the temptation of the Garden of Eden, reborn. And in this twisted retelling, ironic as it is, you are the one being lured. We have no need for this gold as we have more than enough waiting at Shasta. Here lies another tempting promise, one that may yet lead to our undoing if we surrender to its allure." For one agonizing heartbeat, desire and dread waged war in silence, suspended in a moment where both ruin and revelation seemed almost equally inevitable.

No sooner had that moment passed than the carved seraphim wings adorning the Ark began to flicker with searing electric sparks. The chamber shuddered violently as the building energy crescendoed, and a deep, resonant voice boomed: "LET ME OUT!" Ozone filled the air as the unleashed power of the Ark hurled Steve and Elaine to the cold, unyielding stone floor. Amid the chaos and the rising cacophony of collapsing masonry, Elaine cried out, "Better go, Steve!" Instinct and raw terror propelled them to scramble from the disintegrating basement, desperate to escape the cataclysmic surge.

Bursting into the cool night of the trembling hillside, they exited the tunnel and collapsed onto dew-soaked grass as the tumult slowly faded into a fragile, haunted silence. Elaine's voice, heavy with sorrow and reluctant relief, finally broke the quiet: "We solved the mystery—but at what cost?" Steve, gazing toward the slowly brightening horizon, replied in grim resignation, "Some doors aren't meant to be opened, Elaine. Perhaps it's better this way."

As the first reluctant rays of dawn crept over the hills, the ancient heartbeat of Axum and the violent, forbidden secrets they had uncovered receded into a delicate, haunted peace. Each weary step back toward the Nissan Patrol carried with it a truth etched permanently upon their souls—that some mysteries, no matter how tantalizing, are best left shrouded in darkness.

About the Author

Allen Schery has worn many hats in his life. As an archaeologist, he has excavated the Maya ruins at Chichen Itza. As an Anthropologist, he has lived with preliterate groups that starkly contrast with his home culture. After fifty years of mulling over these various experiences, he could finally describe what it means to be a Human Being at any time and culture. Quickly, in six months, a 700-page book, "The Dragon's Breath- the Human Experience," came out of the ether to explain it. Allen has also designed several Museums, including the Corvette Americana Museum in Cooperstown, New York, and published a coffee table book about it. He also did the Dodger Experience Museum at Dodger Stadium in 1999. Also included was the Rose Bowl Museum in Pasadena. Allen is a Dodgers fan and figured out how the Dodgers started in 1883. It took 140 years for this to happen, as many storylines disagreed. Allen searched through the corporate papers from March 1883 on Court Street in Brooklyn and finally found out who these people were. They were gamblers who hid the fact, fearing that such knowledge might affect trust and attendance. He wrote a book entitled "The Boys of Spring-The Birth of the Dodgers."

Allen started collecting Dodger memorabilia in 1952 and never stopped. He has designed a 46,000 square foot museum for the entire 250,000 artifact collection and is currently working on building it. His first university degree was in History, and he has crafted two historical books. One is called "Sanctity and Shadows-The Unholy See." The other is called "The Shattered Cross-The Rise, Fall and Undying Legacy of the Knights Templars." Allen jokingly told people he had not yet discovered what he is good at. He has just finished a book and movie script called "The Mystery of the Ark," which is done in Dan Brown style and loaded with Hitchcockian McGuffin twists that speculate where the Ark has been for 2000 years and what it has been protecting us from.

Index

I ndex

A
Abba Levi, 173
Abba Nevi, 168–69
Addis Ababa, 165–66
Aegean Sea, 7
Alex Weller 87
Allen Schery, 1–2, 172–81
Anthropologist, 181
Arbo, Arbogast 113, 114
Archeology, 4
Ark, 1, 154, 167, 169–70, 173, 175,177, 179, 182
Artemis Patmia, 7, 13
Athens, 164
Axum, 169–71, 173, 175, 179

B

Bahir Dar, 171

Bruce, Halbridge 167–68

C

California gold rush, 113

Cardinal Rausch, 148

Chapel, 136

Chichen Itza, 181

Choking Whisper, 6, 157

Corvette, 103–4, 124, 127–28, 130

Covenant, 167, 173, 177

D

Dead Sea, 39

Diane, 116

E

Edinburgh, 134

Elaine, 107–9, 124–25, 127–30, 133, 142–43, 145–48, 158–60, 162, 164–65, 169, 171, 173, 175, 177–79

Electric Wings Spark, 6, 171

Essenes, 39–40, 43, 48–49, 177

Ethiopia, 160, 162–63, 167, 170

Ethiopia Airlines, 170

F

Father Roberto Samarelli, 173

Father Samarelli, 175

G

Gold Road, 5, 124

H

Hoshiah, 41–42, 48

I

Indiana Jones, 3

J

John, 17–38, 44–51

John Stephen Kopper, 3

Judean Desert, 39

K

Klimkowski Sisters, 106

Koenig, Carl, 171, 174

Kopper, 103–9

M

McCloud Inn, 110, 118
Mount Shasta, 119
Mustang, 113

N

Nissan Patrol, 174–75, 180

P

Patmos, 5, 7, 15–17, 28, 158, 164, 177
Patmos Aktis, 157, 161
Pliny, 17–22, 28–33

Q

Qumran, 5, 28, 39, 41, 43–50, 52, 59, 61

R

Rome, 5, 74, 146–49, 152
Rosslyn Chapel, 6, 142, 144
Ryan Airlines cabin, 150

S

Saint Columba, 147
Santorini, 131, 146, 148–49
Shasta, 103–4, 125, 127, 142, 178
Solomon, 167

Sparks, electric, 179
Springsteen, 125
Star Search, 107
Steve Kopper, 103

T
Tyrrhenian Sea, 74

U
UCLA, 101
UCLA campus, 97

V
Vargas, Victor, 178

Z
Zion, 172

Made in the USA
Monee, IL
29 September 2025